WINTER'S
KISS

WINTER'S KISS

a novella

JENSEN PARKER

Elite Wrestling Entertainment

Made for More Publishing, LLC

WINTER'S KISS

Cover Design: Jensen Parker

Alpha'd: Ashley Vaccaro and Samantha Ivy

Editing: Sophie B. Murphy, Eloquent Inkblot LLC.

ISBN (e-book) : 979-8-9931781-2-7

ISBN (printed) : 979-8-9931781-3-4

Published by Made for More Publishing, LLC.

https://www.jensenparker.com

For my readers,
may all of your Christmas wishes come true.

AUTHOR'S NOTE

Winter's Kiss is a novella in the Elite Wrestling Entertainment Series.

This book contains scenes with discussions of mature subject matter, including on-page physical violence (scripted and non-scripted), on-page sexual content, drinking, and explicit language, and is intended for mature audiences.

Should you need it or have an interest in a more detailed description of certain terms than what is provided in the context of the story, I have included a small glossary in the back of this novella. For a full glossary of wrestling terms, see the back of *Heartbreaker* and the other full-length novels in the series.

- Jensen

Playlist

It's the Most Wonderful Time of the Year - Andy Williams
Plot Twist - Ashley Kutcher
That's So True - Gracie Abrams
Painted Him Perfect - Alexandra Kay
good 4 u - Olivia Rodrigo
Never Sorry - Jeremy Renner
Scars - I Prevail
Rockin' Around the Christmas Tree - Brenda Lee
Outgrown - Dermot Kennedy
that way - Tate McRae
White Horse - Chris Stapleton
'tis the damn season - Taylor Swift
Mirror to the Sky - Jonas Brothers
Straight For The Heart - Alexandra Kay
we can't be friends (wait for you love) - Ariana Grande
It's Beginning to Look Like Christmas - Bing Crosby
Mistletoe - Justin Bieber
Nostalgia - Tate McRae
Deeper Love - Nick Jonas
All I Wanted - Paramore
Burning Down (with Joe Jonas) - Alex Warren
you broke me first - Tate McRae
Both - Ingrid Andress
I Need You Christmas - Jonas Brothers
Santa Tell Me - Ariana Grande
we're not alike - Tate McRae
Wrong Direction - Hailee Steinfeld
Jar of Hearts - Christina Perri
Underneath the Tree - Kelly Clarkson
How You Get the Girl (Taylor's Version) - Taylor Swift
Misery Business - Paramore
Falling For You - Ingrid Andress
Love Somebody Again - Forest Blakk
Like It's Christmas - Jonas Brothers

Apple Music

Spotify

THE CARD

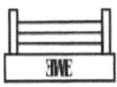 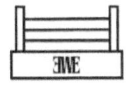

The books in this Series follow characters employed by Elite Wrestling Entertainment, a pro-wrestling company. Below is a list of the wrestlers you'll meet throughout this event, including both their real name and ring name.

Tate Kerrigan - *Kerrigan Tate*
Braxton Powell

Current Roster
John Brooks - *Brooks Taylor*
Savannah Williams - *Savvy Skye*
Brody Wilder - *"The Reaper" Brody Wilder*
Raelynn Carson - *"The Queen of Roses" Rae Rose*
Bennett James - *"The Gladiator" Wolf Bennett*
Colin Montgomery - *Colin Ryker*
Callista Kennedy - *"The Diamond" Cali Kennedy*
Nora Hayes - *Calla Lily*
Emery Russo - *Emmy*
Blair Auden - *Blair Logan*
Zachary Irvine - *Zane Irvine*

EWE Corporate
Amos Rafferty
Chelsea Rafferty
Theo Rafferty
Xander Collins
Tim Cass
Noah Callahan

Media Team
Jude Paul
Scott Harrington
Joanna Valence

PROLOGUE

Tate

WEDNESDAY, NOVEMBER 14, 2012

"You should come!" my friend Jason's bright green eyes sparkle beneath the dim lights of the auditorium. A matching smile spreads across his lips, his head bobbing up and down in a nod. "Live a little."

"You don't have to come if you don't want to, Tate," his older brother's voice rings out. Judah steps through the black curtain from backstage, our boss Terry Wilder at his side. Judah Albright is one of the trainers and the show's general manager at Wilder Wrestling Association. I joined the wrestling school and indie wrestling promotion almost three years ago, and he took me under his wing like the older brother I never had. "I know it's not really your scene."

He's not wrong. Every time I've been invited to join them after shows, I've declined, preferring to go home and rest my aching muscles before I'd have to get up and head to the café for a quick shift before I come here to get my time in the ring.

Tonight, though, I'm feeling a bit...spontaneous. Or maybe it's because I know my best friend is about to bring home her date and put a scrunchie on the door. She said as much this morning. *It's been too damn long, and if he looks anything like his pictures, then I'm going to enjoy it*, she said on her way out the door this morning. I've had six months of peace and quiet since she broke up with her last boyfriend, and I'd rather not have to listen to the sounds of her nightly conquest on the other side of our shared wall.

"No, I want to. It'll be fun," I say before I can change my mind. "I should probably run home and change." Before Farrah brings her date home. "Send me the address and I'll meet you there."

Jason looks at me skeptically.

"Unless you'd prefer I go smelling like a locker room."

"You can borrow some of Ellie's clothes," Jason says with the wave of his hand. Ellie is his girlfriend of four months, and a college student at Utah State. "Her suitcase is still in the car. I just picked her up from the airport."

As nice as the offer is, I'm not sure I'll fit into her clothes. Ellie is at least a few inches shorter than I am, and her boobs are a good size smaller than mine. I guess I could always wear my jeans and one of her—

"Elle, can Tate borrow something to wear from your suitcase?" Jason yells over my shoulder.

"You're coming?" the blonde asks, and I turn to see her walking toward us from the locker room entrance.

I shrug. "I could use the change of scenery."

"Well, you're in luck. I have the cutest dress I bought before the trip, and of course, the one time I don't try it on first, it's too big. But I think it'll fit you!"

"They got you there, Tate," Terry says with a soft chuckle. The older man runs a hand through his graying hair before turning on his heel to return backstage. We do the same, heading for the steel double doors that will lead us out into the real world. Just before we make it out of the auditorium, Terry's voice booms behind us. "But hey! Don't go too wild, though. You have a long weekend ahead of you."

Judah pulls open the thick metal door and motions for me to walk inside the small hallway before reaching around me to open the secondary door. His arm hangs above me, his other hand falling to the small of my back to urge me forward inside the bar. "C'mon, let's get a drink. They should be here in a few," he says after acknowledging the man sitting on a barstool to our right.

The bouncer is tall—I can tell by the height of his bent knees on the stool rungs. He offers a slight nod in my direction before his eyes scan across the room for a quick perimeter sweep.

Not even a minute after we walk away from the bar with beers in hand, Judah pauses in the middle of the room, eyes locked on something straight ahead. He mumbles something I can't hear over the music and conversations around us, but I can tell that whatever he sees, he isn't very happy about it.

"Everything okay?" I ask.

He glances over at me with an unconvincing grin. "Fine."

"You want to try that again?" I laugh behind the opening of my beer.

But he never gets the chance to answer before a hand clasps down on his shoulder, pulling him into an awkward one-armed hug. The other man is shorter than Judah by at least a few inches, with messy brown locks and a sharp smile that lights up beneath the red bulbs strung from the ceiling. He says something to Judah, who rolls his eyes before pulling away from the stranger's grasp. Does he know him? Is this what put him in such a sour mood so suddenly?

"Tate, this is Micah," Judah says without any further explanation. Okay, so he does know him.

The man named Micah rolls his eyes at the lackluster introduction and steps forward. "Micah Evergreen," he says, extending his hand and taking mine when I do the same. He hinges slightly at the waist and brings my knuckles to his lips before pressing a lingering kiss there. The whole thing is a little over the top, but at the same time, I find it kind of cute. When he stands straight, Micah cards a hand through the curled edges of his hair, which hang slightly over his brow, and resets them into the perfect position. "It's lovely to meet you...Tate, was it?"

"Yeah. Are you a friend of Judah and Jason?"

"More Jason, less Judah."

"Not Judah," Judah scoffs from behind him. Typical Judah. He's always the hardest one in the room to please—both professionally and personally. On a normal day, it's one of the things I love most about him, but I'm sure this Micah guy isn't *that* bad if he's friends with Jason. This is just Judah being... Well, Judah. "C'mon, Tate. Jase should be here in a minute. We should—"

"Do you want to go somewhere, and we can talk?" Micah asks, completely ignoring the jab thrown his way. His face lights up with a slow and steady smile I find hard to say no to.

"I'd love to."

He takes my hand and leads me through the crowd in the direction of the booths lining the wall in the back corner. It's quieter over here, and I'm grateful I won't have to yell over the music anymore. Sliding into the only open booth, I notice Jason walk through the front door with Ellie at his side. The younger Albright looks around until he finally sees his brother still standing in the same place I left him. Just before he begins the trek to Judah, another man walks into the bar, and they share a brief handshake with bright smiles. A hearty laugh escapes the newcomer before he follows Jason through the crowd, and only seconds after they reach their destination do all eyes turn toward me.

There's a tug of familiarity when I make eye contact with this new man, but I know I've never met him before. His gaze narrows past me before he shakes his head, turning away from me.

"Tate," Micah says, drawing my attention back to him.

"I'm sorry, what did you say?"

He laughs, taking my hand back into his and drawing smaller circles on the pulse point of my wrist. "I said, tell me about yourself. What do you do for work?"

1

Tate

MONDAY, DECEMBER 16, 2019

SEVEN YEARS LATER

"And still the EWE Women's Tag Team champions: Blair Logan and Emmy!" The ring announcer's voice rings out through the arena. He draws out the last syllable of *Emmy*'s name for dramatic effect.

My own tag team partner climbs back into the ring, draping her arm over my shoulders as we watch our opponents stalk backward up the ramp. The women smirk, titles raised over their heads, before *Blair* blows a kiss and waves while *Emmy* pretends to rub her fist into her eye as if she were crying.

"You okay?" my partner asks over the noise of the crowd. "Pretty hard hit you took."

"Fine," I say, waving her off before rolling underneath the bottom rope.

The video package for the following match—*"The Hurricane" Aaron Zimmerman* vs. *Zane Irvine*—begins, draping the arena in darkness except for the glow of the oversized TV screens. My partner Savannah—better known to these people as *Savvy Skye*—touches hands with fans around the barricade as we walk backstage, and normally, I'd follow suit, but the dull ache in my temple begs me to get to the back as soon as possible. Whether it's from the jet lag after the two-week European tour we just finished or the hit to the head I just took, I'm not sure, but I'm fine...or I'll be fine...I think.

Stepping through the curtain into gorilla—the central operations station of our entire program—I vaguely glance at Noah Callahan over the top of his monitor. The Chief Content Officer doesn't look away from the screen, saying something into the mouthpiece of his headset before giving me a thumbs-up. I'll take it, because it's better than the alternative. I keep walking, even when Savannah stops to talk to Noah, just like always. They're close—in fact, Noah is one of the only reasons the "*Queen of the Ring*" decided to return to EWE in the first place. So, I never bother to interrupt their conversations because, who knows, maybe it'll lead to something good for me while I'm her on-screen counterpart.

"Oh my gosh, Tate!" Emmy yells as I step through the curtain into the hallway. The devilish grin of the character she plays on-screen is replaced by genuine concern. "I swear, I didn't mean to hit you that hard. Are you okay? I'm so sorry."

"I heard you hit the ground from the other side of the ring," Blair adds, adjusting the title on her shoulder.

During the match, Emmy swiped my legs off the apron, and it should've been an easy stunt, but her swing pulled my legs out too far. I went down hard, hitting the edge of the apron first, and then falling to the ground. The landing was less than optimal; my hands took most of the impact, but my head and the ground still collided harder than I would've preferred.

"I'll be fine," I say, rubbing the sore part of my neck. "Nothing a little Icy Hot, Tylenol, and maybe a massage can't fix."

And maybe a hot bath when I make it to Nashville. I roll

out my shoulders and crane my neck from side to side, finding some relief after a quick pop in the space between my neck and shoulder.

"You sure? You could always use it as your excuse not to go next week," Savannah says, finally joining us from gorilla.

I scoff. "You know Farrah would *never* let me out of it. I could be on my deathbed, and she'd find someone to wheel me down the aisle."

"What's next week?" Blair asks.

"My best friend is getting married on Christmas."

The other two women swoon, and Emmy sighs dreamily. "That's so romantic. I'd love a Christmas wedding."

"Yeah, it's going to be something. This has been her biggest dream since we were kids, so I have no doubt it'll be the most lavish spectacle you can imagine." At least, it would have been if her parents were funding the whole thing. Apparently, they only offered to pay for the venue, which seemed very unlike them, but Farrah wasn't very forthcoming with the details. In fact, I would've never known if she hadn't accidentally mentioned it on the phone a few months ago.

"Isn't it going to be a little weird, though?" Savannah asks, twisting her long brown hair into a loose ponytail before letting it fall down her back. "I mean, she's marrying your ex-boyfriend."

"Wait a damn minute," Blair says, looking at me like I have three heads. "She's marrying your *ex-boyfriend*?"

I glare over at my tag team partner as we begin to walk down the hallway, but her only response is a simple shrug. Savannah tries to hide it, but I see the slight tug on the opposite side of her mouth.

"And you're going?" Blair continues.

"The breakup was mutual," I say with my own shrug. "Dating a wrestler isn't exactly what he had pictured for his happily ever after."

Blair and Emmy continue to look back and forth between me and each other. This isn't the first time I've received a response like this. Most people think I'm crazy for staying friends with Farrah, and sometimes, I wonder if they're right.

"Micah wanted something a little more...reliable," I say, earning a scoff from Savannah. I glare at her. "Someone who could be there for date night on a random Tuesday, someone who'd be there when he got home from work every night. Farrah's a teacher. She's planted roots in our hometown... She's *there*, and I'm...not."

"Were they messing around behind your back?" Emmy asks, a touch of pity in her words.

I laugh, but a familiar pit forms in my stomach. The one that always forms when someone asks me this question. "No, nothing like that."

"Are you sure?"

"Positive," I say with a smile, but I can tell they still don't believe me. Hell, I don't believe me. The thought has crossed my mind on more than one occasion since Farrah and Micah got together, but I've never admitted it to anyone, not even my own family.

My lack of admission has never stopped other people from voicing their opinions, though, including the woman standing beside me, who I've grown close to over the last three months. Savannah Williams—or rather, *Savvy Skye*—is the first person most people think of when they talk about women's wrestling. She is this generation's *Holly Graham* or *Jolene Briggs*, two of the greatest from the previous generation. Savannah has helped open so many doors for women in this industry throughout her tenure, but I never got the chance to meet her when I first moved up to the main roster because she left the company unexpectedly. When she returned earlier this year, I never imagined Savannah would tell me she was impressed with what she'd seen of my work over the years, let alone that I'd get to work beside her and learn from her.

"You're a saint," Blair says over her shoulder, holding the locker room door open. "There's no way I'd be okay with my best friend dating my ex."

"Because you're still in love with him," Emmy scoffs at her best friend.

"I am not!"

"That's not what you said two weeks ago, Miss If-Knox-Wanted-To-I'd-Get-Back-Together."

"Hey!" Blair gasps, eyes wide. "I told you that in confidence."

Emmy rolls her eyes before she turns to dig through her bag for a change of clothes.

Blair glares at her best friend for a moment longer before changing the subject back to my current predicament. "Regardless, if my best friend tried to date my ex-boyfriend, I'd drop her like a hot potato."

"Good thing I'd never go after Knox Campbell, then," Emmy says, examining a pair of leggings.

"Why do you say it like that?" Blair asks, her nose wrinkling. Emmy gives her a knowing look before returning to her hunt for a top this time. "Why do you say it like *that*?"

"The same reason I told you not to call him when you were drunk off your ass the other night."

Blair rolls her eyes. She zips up her bag in one swift motion and hikes the strap over her shoulder, heading for the door. "I'll see you ladies tomorrow." She leaves without a word to her best friend, and I share an awkward glance with Savannah after she pulls a sweater over her head. It must be her fiancé's, with the way it swallows her whole, the bottom hem falling below her ass. She lifts a brow before shaking her head, turning back to the mirror to fix her hair.

"Everything okay there, Em?" I ask.

"I think it's just the holidays making her sentimental," Emmy says, pushing her legs through the clean pair of leggings.

"It's understandable," Savannah says, zipping her own bag.

"Says the girl engaged to her dream guy."

Savannah laughs but doesn't deny it. Her *dream guy*, as Emmy called him, is none other than Brooks Taylor. Around here, we just call him Brooks, but to Savannah and the government, he's John. He's the face of not just our company, but professional wrestling, and together they make one hell of a power couple. "It hasn't exactly been sunshine and rainbows," she says, pulling the sleeves of the sweatshirt down and clutching the ends in her hands. "But I can sympathize with her. When John and I broke up, it was around Christmas, and after spending practically ten years of holidays together, it was rough. This is Blair's first year without him. Give her some grace, Em."

"Yeah, I guess." Emmy sighs. "I'd better go before she leaves me."

"Good luck!" I yell after her when she walks out the door.

Normally, we'd all be headed home to rest and recover for two days before we'd need to be back in the ring on Thursday night. However, this week we have nonstop tapings because we're off for the next two weeks. Say what you want about our schedule, but at least the company is considerate enough to give us Christmas off.

"Okay, what did I miss?" a raven-haired woman asks when she walks into the locker room. Raelynn Carson, or "*Queen of Roses*" *Rae Rose*, is another veteran who joined EWE around the same time as Savannah. She glances between me, her best friend, and the door. "First, Blair goes storming past me a few minutes ago, and now Emmy?"

"Don't ask," Savannah says, threading the handle of her suitcase through the trolley sleeve of her matching duffel bag.

"I thought they were done fighting."

"Are they ever done fighting?" I ask and can't help but

laugh. While Emmy and Blair might be best friends—hell, they even wrestled together in the Ohio indies before being called up to EWE together—they always seem to be at odds with one another.

I pull out my phone, scrolling through the notifications from a family group chat, then a few separate messages from my sister, mom, and one from my neighbor. Nothing out of the ordinary, except for the one missed call from ten minutes ago.

1 Missed Call: Braxton Powell

Braxton Powell?

What is he calling for? I haven't seen or heard from Braxton in...shit, I don't even know how long. At least three years. He's Farrah's ex-boyfriend and the ex-best friend of her now fiancé. He and Micah had a falling out well before Farrah left Braxton, but according to her, finding out she and Micah had started dating was the final nail in the coffin. Their friendship had been rocky for a while. I can't say for sure what drove the initial wedge between them, but it started after Jason's untimely death in a car accident, only a few months after Micah and I started dating.

Why would he call me? Surely, it can't be anything more than a butt-dial.

"Tate," Raelynn's voice catches my attention. I look up from my phone, still a little confused about the missed call. "You zoned out pretty hard. Everything okay?"

"Sorry," I say, running a hand through my hair. "I just got a call from Farrah's ex-boyfriend."

Savannah's eyes widen, and she immediately sits in the chair across from me. "Wait, her ex-boyfriend called you?"

"Yeah," I say, staring down at the dark screen. "I haven't talked to him since well before they broke up. Why would he be calling me?"

"The ex-boyfriend of your best friend who's marrying

your ex-boyfriend on Christmas Day?" Raelynn asks, and I nod. "Wait! What if he's trying to recruit you to stop the wedding?"

"He'd know better."

"Tate, he just called you a week before the wedding. It's the only logical explanation. Hey! Don't roll your eyes," Raelynn says when she catches her best friend doing just that.

"It's not the only explanation," Savannah counters. "But it is pretty suspicious."

The smirk that crosses Rae's face tells me I'm not sure I'm going to like what's about to come out of her mouth. "Is he cute?"

Her best friend sighs, pinching the bridge of her nose and shaking her head. "Rae."

"What? I'm just curious!" Raelynn looks back at me. "Were you ever into him? Clearly, your best friend was into your man. Were you into hers?"

"No!" I scoff, and I'm not surprised when their brows raise at the same time. That wasn't very convincing. "Not while they were together, anyway. But that doesn't mean anything."

"What if he's calling to ask you out? You should call him back. Find out what he wants," Raelynn says.

Calling to ask me out? I think she's taken one too many hits to the head recently, or she's more of a romantic than I thought. However, her idea dares to crack open the door I had pushed any thought of Braxton behind before I'd shut it, locked it, and thrown away the key a long time ago. Braxton wasn't the man I was supposed to be thinking about back then.

Savannah's brow arches again. "And if he's calling because he wants to crash the wedding, then what?"

"Then she tells the bride and groom! At least they'll know ahead of time."

I glance back down at my phone, tapping the screen, and

his name stares back at me. A knot forms in my stomach. "Should I tell Farrah?"

Raelynn starts to answer but stops herself.

"Well, don't hold back now," Savannah says.

"I know you're going to disagree with me."

"And that's stopped you before?" Savannah's face scrunches, and I can't help but laugh. This is how they always are, but I guess that's what happens when you've been friends for over a decade. It reminds me a lot of how Farrah and I used to be.

"I don't think you should tell her. No reason to cause her more stress," Raelynn finally says with a shrug. "Weddings are...exhausting. Take it from someone who has helped two sisters plan their weddings and is about to start planning her own."

"Don't forget mine," Savannah adds.

"Oh yes, the Brooks Taylor-Savvy Skye extravaganza next year. How could I forget?" Raelynn giggles.

Savannah rolls her eyes but can't fight her smile. "I agree with Rae. Why tell her when it's only going to cause potential problems? And like you said, Tate, it might not even mean anything."

"Who are you and what have you done with my best friend? Should I call John and tell him something is wrong with you?"

"Oh, shut up."

"Yeah—Yeah, you're right, Sav. It was probably just a butt-dial. No sense in telling her when it doesn't mean anything," I say with a small smile. Was it really just a butt dial? I don't know—it seems almost too random—but it sounds better than the alternative. What if he is trying to stop the wedding? How am I supposed to handle this?

2

Tate

SATURDAY, DECEMBER 21, 2019

I should get up and take a shower...Should pack for my trip back home to Snowhaven Springs. It's a small town in the northeastern part of Utah, settled near the base of the Bear River Mountains—one of those places you probably wouldn't know existed unless you knew. Around this time of year, it's what I imagine the North Pole looks like. The gingerbread architecture of downtown is only amplified by the colorful lights outlining the buildings, wreaths and garland hung between rooftops, red ribbon and bows tied around each lamp post, and small Christmas trees with simple decor on every corner, so as not to overshadow the large one in the town square, with an ice rink installed beside it. Add snow, and it looks like a scene from any Christmas movie you can imagine.

I *should* get up and shower. I should finally unpack from the last week on the road and repack for my trip back home... but then, the same thought I've had about a hundred times crosses my mind. *Am I actually about to stand up in the wedding of my best friend and my ex-boyfriend*? It hadn't actually hit me until I got home yesterday, when there wasn't anything to distract me from what is sure to be the most awkward Christmas of my life. Instead of dealing with it, though, I crawled into bed and haven't moved since, except for collecting the food I had delivered earlier. But every chance it gets, the same thought creeps into my mind, making me wonder why I agreed to be Farrah's bridesmaid. Not just a bridesmaid, but the maid of honor.

It's not like I want Micah back, but I suppose I haven't actually had to face the truth about their relationship before now. Because until now, I haven't been around them often. My career keeps me on the road the majority of the year, and when I'm not on the road, I'm here...in Tampa, not Snowhaven Springs.

When Farrah called me two years ago to tell me she had broken up with Braxton, I was shocked and confused. What did she mean? It had only been a month since he got down on one knee and asked her to be his wife. Why would she end things so suddenly? Had Braxton been hiding some alter ego all those years? Did he flip the switch once he felt comfortable enough? That couldn't be it. Micah, maybe, but Braxton? No chance.

"There's someone else," she said over the line.

I sat upright on the locker room bench. "What do you mean, *someone else*?"

"Tate...I, uh, I never meant for it to happen, and I don't want to hurt you, but you've been broken up for over a year, and—"

My stomach sank with every word she uttered. "Micah?" I practically spat out the name. "You're *fucking* my ex-boyfriend?"

I thought he'd left town? I'd heard through the grapevine—aka my mom and her gossipy friends—Micah had disappeared about two months after we broke up the year before. Rumor had it his parents shipped him off to rehab on the other side of the country. Seemed far-fetched to me, especially after the way they reacted when I begged them for help, but if it was true, I was happy he was getting help.

Farrah huffed on the other end. "You don't have to say it like *that*. We ran into him at the store last month, and even though Braxton isn't the least bit concerned about where his best friend has been the last ten months, I am. I went to check in on him every couple of days, and the next thing I knew..."

"You fucked him."

"Can you please stop saying it like that? You make it sound dirty."

I scoffed. "Well, what would you prefer I call it, Fay? You just admitted you slept with another man while you were still with your fiancé!"

"We didn't..." Farrah sighed. "We didn't sleep together. Not until...Well, that's beside the point."

"Then what is the point?" I asked, pinching the bridge of my nose as I paced the length of the locker room. I had just finished competing in a battle royale to win the number one contender's spot for the Elite Wrestling Entertainment Women's Championship. This was the last conversation I wanted to be having. "Farrah, to be quite honest with you, I don't care if you want to date Micah. You don't need my permission. However, I do care if you hurt Braxton in the process."

"Oh! What a relief. I thought you were going to be upset with me for—" Farrah continued to ramble on, detailing how things had come to pass, but expertly avoiding any mention of the man whose heart she'd just ripped out and stepped on.

I blame myself for how things turned out, really. I had decided to move across the country and follow my dreams, but Micah refused to uproot his life from our small town. My choice to accept the job at EWE meant moving to Florida—

over two thousand miles from home—and it changed everything. I saw the writing on the wall a few months in, but for some reason, we continued to hold on to our relationship for almost two years. I don't know why. For me, I think part of my reluctance to let go was because it was like having a little piece of home on the rare occasion he visited, or maybe because I was comfortable in the confines of our partnership. Not to mention, I felt like I owed it to Jason to *try*. He wouldn't have introduced us if he didn't think we'd make a good pair.

A subtle vibration from deep within the sea of blankets catches my attention. *I swear, if this is Farrah calling me about—Oh, shit.* The name on the screen makes my stomach lurch, and the pork bao I finished less than five minutes ago begins to crawl its way back up my throat. When he didn't call again after Monday, I assumed it had been a butt-dial. But now...here he is...calling again.

I stare at it until the screen goes black.

Should I call back? No, Sav and Rae said no. I should leave it alone. They're right. Right? I don't want to—

My phone dings with a notification. *1 New Voicemail.*

"Shit," the word comes out in a low hiss under my breath. I know I shouldn't, but I can't help myself. I pause the television before pressing play on the message.

There's a brief moment of silence before...

"Hey, Tay." His voice floods me with a nostalgic warmth. The rough-around-the-edges texture scratches at my surface, already wearing down my resolve. His voice has always been stoic, with a quiet intensity that carries a no-nonsense demeanor, the complete opposite of his former best friend. And hearing it for the first time in years raises goosebumps across my skin and warms me from the inside out.

He hasn't called me Tay in...years. The nickname stems from my government name: Taylor. At first, I hated it, but over the years, I had grown accustomed to it from him, and only him. Braxton and I had gotten close through our shared connection with Micah and Jason. We picked on each other and pushed each other's buttons, until ultimately one of us—usually him—would finally surrender. Micah found us annoying, Jason found us entertaining, but it was Farrah who struggled to accept our friendship. When she officially came into the picture as Braxton's girlfriend, she didn't like how comfortable her boyfriend seemed with another woman, even if that woman was her best friend.

"I, uh, I know this is weird—really weird," Braxton's voice says on the recording. "But...I need you. I need your help. I think Farrah is about to make a big mistake."

And there it is.

"I think you might be the only person she'll listen to."

He's joking, right? Farrah won't listen to me. She's been planning for this moment for as long as I've known her. She had the scrapbooks and the magazine cutouts, and she had her dream date narrowed down to the exact time: Christmas Day at two-thirty in the afternoon. There was no way she was going to let anyone or anything get in the way.

"I know it's been a long time, but I really need to talk to you. Please call me back."

The call disconnects, and silence envelops me again. I stare at the phone for a moment longer, at his name, and I almost let my thumb press down on it. But I know I shouldn't, not after what I just heard...Instead, I scroll until I find Farrah, but I can't bring myself to call her, either. That sounds like a nightmare. She has already called me ten times today about things going awry in Wedding Land, calling me back five minutes later each time once things calmed down and had been fixed. From here, I can mute her out, but I know as soon as I arrive, the other bridesmaids are going to tag me in. They've had a front row seat to her meltdowns for months, while I've been on the sidelines on the other side of the country. I'm not sure I want to put myself in the middle of it any sooner than I have to.

You know what? I'm just going to ignore it. There's no reason I have to say anything now. Whatever he wants to talk about can wait until after the bride and groom say *I do* on Wednesday afternoon.

My phone vibrates again, but only once this time.

> **Braxton Powell**
> SLC Coffee Co. tomorrow @ 9am.

Is he really asking me to meet him tomorrow when I get into town? That's a bit bold, considering anyone could see us and report it back to Farrah, which is something I don't want to deal with. Still, he's going to great lengths to talk to me about this. The Braxton I once knew was an honorable person. He'd never try to stop a wedding if he didn't think there was cause to do so...What has him asking for my help to do just that?

Normally, I'd try to stave off my curiosity, tell myself to ignore it and move on, but today is not that day.

> Bold of you to assume I'll be in town by then.

> **Braxton Powell**
> Oh, so you ARE getting these? I was starting to think maybe you'd changed your number or had me blocked.

> We need to talk, Tay.

> About what?

In person.

I'm not helping you stop
this wedding.

Bold of you to
assume that's what
I'm trying to do.

I don't believe you.

9am.

"So bossy," I murmur, tossing my phone on the bed. It annoys me that he still knows me well enough to assume I'll be in town so early. I was notorious for catching the red-eye flight even before I worked at EWE. Most of my coworkers fly in to whatever city we're occupying the night before a show, but not me. I'd rather stay home and enjoy my own bed for as long as possible. Has it given me a few close calls? Sure, but I think it's worth it.

I huff and cross my arms, glancing at the phone. Part of me waits for the screen to light up again with another text message, but it never does.

Meeting Braxton is crossing into enemy territory, and if we get caught...I'm screwed. Farrah will never let me hear the end of it. Farrah's mother will never let me hear the end of it. Hell, *my* mother will never let me hear the end of it. But he's so damn persistent. What is so important that he has to call and text multiple times now?

I groan, picking up my phone. Fine, I'll go, but only because I want to know what is so damn important.

And maybe a small part of me wants to see him again. I respond with:

Make it 10.

3

Tate

SUNDAY, DECEMBER 22, 2019

SLC Coffee Co. is a local coffee shop on the outskirts of downtown Salt Lake City, a hidden gem the locals can still enjoy without being inundated by tourists—though I'm surprised they haven't found it yet. With its dark walls, dimmed string bulbs draped from the wooden beams on the ceiling, and exposed brick behind the counter and lining the windowsills, it's every coffee influencer's dream.

Kicking the snow off my boots, I survey the landscape of the street to ensure there isn't anyone I might know lurking around. Salt Lake City isn't far from Snowhaven, and I can't be sure Farrah hasn't sent someone on an errand down to the city. She wouldn't care if it's an hour and a half both ways to get down here. The last thing I need is for one of her minions—Bethany, Katie, and Morgan—to report back that they saw me in town and I hadn't come straight to the resort. Or worse, they saw me with Braxton.

I spot him the moment I walk in the door. He's situated in the far corner, his chin tucked in slightly as he skims a newspaper. I force the small quirk in the corner of my lips back down. He looks good, better than he did the last time I saw him, because he looks more like himself. I swim through the small crowd lined up in front of the counter, and as much as I'd like to place an order, I don't plan on being here very long. I need to get on the road before Farrah realizes what time it is.

Reaching the table, I shrug out of my coat and slide into the chair across from him. Braxton doesn't lift his attention from the paper; his eyes glide from left to right, and his tongue pokes out of the right corner. He briefly glances up under his lashes, and the twinkle in his hazel eyes brings a flash of heat to my cheeks before he returns to the article without a word.

You've got to be kidding. I huff, falling back into my chair even further and crossing my arms and legs.

After a moment, Braxton folds the paper in half and then again until it's a small rectangle, and I can see the name across the top: *Snowhaven Gazette.*

"Anything good?"

"Depends on what you consider good," he says.

The barista calls out his name before he stalks up to the counter. He returns with two coffees—Two? Why does he have—

"I take it you still drink it black, with an ice cube or two?"

He remembers? I don't answer but take the cup from him anyway. Why does he remember that?

"How was the flight in?" Braxton asks.

Is he really asking me about my flight? This isn't some casual meetup. He's the one who called me because he *had* to tell me something. We're not here to catch up over coffee. Why not just get to the damn point?

"What are we doing here, Braxton?" I ask, resisting the urge to look at my watch. I'm going to be late, and I can guarantee it will raise questions. Questions I don't feel like answering.

He stares at me for a moment, eyes locked on mine with a look I can't quite decipher. The distance we've put between us still feels foreign even after all these years. Everything in me yearns to be wrapped in his warm embrace and hear his hearty laughter. To be the friends we once were before Farrah decided our friendship was a threat to their relationship, that I was a threat to their relationship. Braxton finally breaks his gaze, hands tightening around his mug. He stares down into the black liquid for a few heartbeats before he takes a deep breath and lifts his gaze again. "He came to me for money."

My heart sinks in my chest.

"I haven't..." Braxton scoffs. "I haven't heard from the fucker in years, and last week, he called me, asking me for a loan."

"Braxton, please tell me you're joking," I say, voice no louder than a whisper. This cannot be happening. Not now. Not again.

"I wish I could, Tay."

"No, it's not...It can't be. He got help, he went to—"

"You sure?" Braxton asks, brow cocked over his coffee mug as he takes a sip. What is that supposed to mean?

"Um, hi," a small voice interrupts us. Turning my head, I meet the eyes of a young girl who can't be more than ten. She looks directly at me with a sheepish smile. "I'm sorry,"—she glances over at Braxton—"but can I have a picture, *Kerrigan*?"

Kerrigan, as in the *"Ice Princess" Kerrigan Tate*—my in-ring persona. Obviously, she's an EWE fan, and part of me wants to decline the girl's request, but the look on her face makes it nearly impossible.

I offer Braxton an apologetic smile.

He merely shrugs and leans back in his chair with a smile. Throughout the whole interaction—conversation, photo, and a quick hug—I feel his steady gaze on me. When the girl turns to him to apologize for the second time, he still holds his smile. "Anytime, sweetie," he assures her behind another sip of coffee.

When she's gone, I sigh. "I'm so sorry."

"No apology needed, Tay. It was pretty cool."

"You might be the only person who thinks so," I say with a slight scoff.

His response is a breath of fresh air compared to what I'm used to from almost everyone else in my life, but no one more than Micah. He used to get pissed when people recognized me outside of the ring, hated *his* time being interrupted when he already got so little of it—by choice, I might add. On one hand, I understood. We didn't get a lot of time together, but he didn't want to travel to Florida, and public interactions were part of the job…What was I supposed to do? I couldn't ignore people who made sure I got paid every week.

Braxton takes another sip of coffee, still gripping the mug even after he sets it down. His nail traces the white porcelain handle. "Sad to see you drop the belt at Beachbash. I was hoping they'd let you keep it a little longer."

"Since when do you watch wrestling?"

"I watch occasionally…and my brother-in-law is obsessed with it. He's what people in the business call a…What is it again? A *mark*?"

"Yeah, marks." I laugh. A "mark" is the term those of us in the business use to refer to the more…passionate fans. The ones who believe everything they see on screen. "Does he really believe everything is—"

"No, he knows, but he chooses to ignore that fact while he's watching it every week."

"A lot of people do. Hell, I catch myself doing it sometimes. It's fun to let loose and just enjoy every once in a while."

"I have yet to tell him we used to be friends."

Used to be friends. That stings. I bite down on the corner of my lip, tracing the length of my mug with my fingertip.

Bringing it to my lips, I ask, "Macie didn't tell him?"

A single *ha* passes his lips after he swallows his own drink. "Are you kidding? My sister would like to preserve some of her sanity. She adores Max and his love for it, but if he found out we knew someone in the business..." Braxton shakes his head with a small, affectionate smile. "Well, let's just say, she'd probably kill me if I told him."

I laugh, and his mouth lifts into a full-blown smile, complete with the wrinkles in the corners of his eyes. A familiar air settles around us, and it makes me nostalgic for the old days before life tore our friendship apart. Braxton was one of my closest friends for a short time, and I had to remind myself of that when I started to have feelings for him outside the realm of friendship. I told myself it was only a crush, and only because we had grown so close in such a short amount of time. We spent a lot of time together because not only was he my friend, but he was also Micah's best friend. And I was happy with Micah...At least that's what I told myself. Looking back, I see it now, all the signs pointing toward what was to come, but I held on for as long as I could. I thought that's what Jason wanted. I thought I would be letting him down if I didn't make it work. Sometimes I wish I'd listened to my gut instinct sooner...

My smile falls quickly when I catch sight of the newspaper again. This time, I can make out the corner of my best friend's head folded in half by the crease. Reality slaps me in the face, reminding me why we're sitting here in the first place, and it's not just for two old friends to catch up over coffee. "Did he say why he needed the money?" I ask.

Now, Braxton's face falls. "Just said he was a bit short for the wedding."

"That doesn't mean—"

"Why else would he be short, Taylor?"

We're using my government name now?

Braxton continues, "Why not go to their parents? Why come to me?"

Those are the same questions I asked myself when Farrah called me two months ago. She asked for a loan, saying Micah was waiting on some money to come in from a private client.

"You know something," he says, head tilting slightly. *Shit.* "Did he come to *you*, too?"

I shake my head. "Farrah."

"You're fucking joking. Tate—"

"About two months ago. She asked me for a loan because Micah was waiting for some money to come in. I don't—"

"Did she pay you back?" Braxton's gaze is intense from the other side of the table. I don't want to answer, but I don't have to because my lack of response is answer enough. "Tay, c'mon. You gotta see what's right in front of you."

"So, what if he is?" I ask. "Farrah obviously doesn't care, because she—"

"Or she doesn't know."

Of course, she knows. She has to know. I sit back in my seat, crossing my arms over my chest, and narrow my gaze. "So, what, you're going to ride in on your white horse, tell her the truth, and hope she falls into your waiting arms? That's not going to happen, Bray."

His jaw sets. "I don't want her back."

I scoff. "Okay. Then why are you doing this?"

"I have my reasons."

"Okay, I think we're done here," I say, pushing up from my chair. "I'm not going to be part of these games, Braxton. You're better than this. Find someone else to help you win back the heart of the woman who never wanted you in the first place."

I grab my car keys off the table, refusing to meet his stare that I feel burning through me. I can't stand to see the reaction I just warranted from him. It was a low blow. I know it was, and it's one I'm not even sure is true.

Did Farrah leave him for Micah? Yes. Was it fair to basically say she settled for Braxton instead? No. Even if it is true, Farrah would never admit to it. Not with my history with Micah.

Tugging my jacket over my arms, I swim through the crowd, and just as I walk out the door, my phone rings. When I dig it out of my pocket, I glance at the screen: *Farrah*. Right on cue.

4

"This cannot be happening," I whisper the moment I round the corner into the resort lobby. It's a grand space, complete with an oversized floor-to-ceiling stone fireplace, a large sitting area, bookshelves, and a boutique convenience store in the left corner. Skylights and the windows along the back wall allow the last remaining minutes of sunlight to cast a warm glow on the space before the dimmed lights inside take over.

Why is he here?

Dumb question. I know why he's here. I just wish he wasn't.

Farrah could walk around the corner at any second, and the last thing I need is for her to see him standing there. I've spent all day putting out the fires she was too stressed to handle, including the biggest one of all: her mother. You'd think Mrs. Frost was the one getting married with how worked up she's been. But I think this particular fire standing right in front of me is one even I can't manage.

Braxton leans against the front desk, casually chatting with the front desk clerk. They are both so engrossed in whatever the topic of discussion is that they don't notice me. The clerk's hands fly through the air as he tells a story, and they share a hearty laugh. Then, Braxton's stare meets my own, and I hope I look as annoyed as I feel. Something tells me I don't, because his smile never fails. In fact, it only seems to grow bigger. His eyes light up with a familiar spark of recognition. He slaps his hand down on the counter, says something to his counterpart, and excuses himself.

"What in the hell are you doing here?" I hiss when we meet in the center of the lobby.

"Figured you needed this," Braxton says, lifting my purse by the strap in his right hand.

Upon my arrival at the resort, I realized I'd left my purse at the coffee shop. Somehow, I managed to snag my keys and phone off the table, but forgot the other most important thing. When I called the shop, they said no one had turned anything in, which meant one of two things: one, someone had stolen it, or two, Braxton had it. And I wasn't calling him after the way our conversation ended.

My purse dangles in the space between us, but I don't reach for it.

"Or not, I can keep it if you—" Braxton chuckles when I finally snatch it from his hand, but he doesn't let go. "We still need to finish our conversation."

"Brax—"

"I need your help, Tay. You're the only person she'll listen to."

I laugh. "Have you met Farrah? She doesn't listen to *anyone*. And after the last five hours, I can promise you, there's nothing worth impeding her course now. Not even you...Especially not you."

"She'll listen to you! You're her best friend, her only real friend, and she knows you won't bring something like this up unless you have reason to believe—"

"I don't have reason to believe."

"Taylor."

"Braxton."

He sighs. "You said it yourself. Farrah asked you for money not long ago because he was waiting on money to come in. How many times have you heard that excuse before?"

Too many.

Too many times I've heard the same excuse, but I don't need to tell him that.

Micah and I never commingled funds when we were together, but there were plenty of times he asked me for a small loan. The first few times, he paid me back, but after the fifth or sixth time, he stopped. He always promised he'd get it back to me, but he was waiting for this "one big client" to pay...That excuse never made sense to me—he was paid a salary—but what do I know? When it wasn't good enough for me anymore, when I finally refused to lend (I use that term loosely) him money, Micah got angry. He said things—mean things—and stormed out, disappearing for two days.

That's when I called Braxton. It had been months since I'd seen him or talked to him one-on-one because of Farrah's jealousy. I knew if she found out, I'd have to face the consequences, but I didn't care. I needed help, and he was the only person I felt like I could turn to. He told me about the gambling problem that Micah had supposedly kicked to the curb, but it seemed to me that he was back on the boat. Braxton made me go to Micah's parents, but they weren't interested in hearing about something he'd eventually lose interest in. "Just like last time," they said.

"Did you tell her about his problem before?" Braxton asks, pulling me back to the present. "She never said anything to me, but—"

"No," I say, shaking my head. "I didn't tell anyone. Not

after his parents brushed it off."

"You have to tell her, Tay."

"She'll never believe me, Braxton. If anything, she's going to think I'm—"

"Tate?" I hear my name from behind me. As if this couldn't get any worse, the exact thing I feared has come to fruition. "Oh, thank goodness. I thought you had already— Oh! Braxton?" Farrah joins us, blue eyes wide as she stares between us, and then at our hands still connected by my purse strap. "What are you doing here?"

"He was just leaving," I say, tugging on the strap, and this time he lets go.

Braxton chuckles, eyes never leaving mine. "Yeah, I was just leaving...Sorry for the intrusion, Farrah. I was just returning Tay's purse." He finally drops my gaze, flashing a brief smile at his ex-girlfriend.

Farrah's narrowed eyes relax, and a Cheshire grin splits her face in two. "Wait, are you...are you guys together?"

We answer at the same time, with completely different responses. My *what*? Is met by his *yes*. Braxton steps forward, wrapping his arm around my shoulders and tugging me close. He ignores the glare I shoot up at him, thumb caressing my shoulder through the fabric of my sweatshirt.

Farrah squeals, and it echoes through the open space. "Oh my gosh! Tate, why didn't you tell me?"

"Because we're not—"

"I always knew you liked each other. It was so, *so* obvious. I can't believe you didn't tell me! This is so wonderful."

As if this interaction couldn't get any worse, the groom struts out of the elevator hallway and immediately heads our way. This is the first time I've seen him since my arrival, but I know exactly where he's been because before I could even ask—not that I planned to—Mrs. Frost complained to me about how Micah was on the slopes with some of the boys. I'd be a liar if I said my thoughts didn't immediately return to the conversation I'd had with Braxton earlier. Was Micah really on the slopes, or was he doing something else?

I watch his eyes narrow as he gets closer and recognizes the other person standing beside me. Micah doesn't try to hide his displeasure, immediately asking, "What in the hell are *you* doing here?"

"Don't be rude, Mick," Farrah chides.

"I just asked a damn question." Micah surveys the scene, and under his scrutinizing stare, I shrink back into Braxton's side. He gives me a gentle, reassuring squeeze. *I'm here*, it says, and it's more than Micah ever gave me in an uncomfortable situation. Example: meeting his parents for the first time. They had been less than enthused to learn their son was dating a wrestler. That fact immediately tanked their first impressions of me, and Micah left me to tread water on my own.

"I was just bringing Tay her bag. She forgot it this morning," Braxton says.

"This morning?" Farrah asks with an arched brow. "That's why you were late! You were trying to get a quickie in before having to be here all weekend. Why didn't you just—"

"That is not what happened," I say, but she's not convinced.

My best friend chuckles. "All you had to say was you wanted a few minutes with your boyfriend, Tate."

"Oh, for the love of God." I glare up at Braxton, who only wears an amused grin. He's enjoying this way too much.

"Boyfriend?" Micah practically chokes on the word. "You're dating?"

"I know, I can't believe they didn't tell us!" Farrah swoons, and it seems weird to me how well she's taking this news. For someone who was dead set on keeping me and Braxton apart, she's very...excited. "Isn't it so funny how things work out?"

Micah scoffs, refusing to look away from me. "Yeah, funny."

"I'm sorry, I didn't mean to keep her this morning, but I had to make sure she got coffee. You know how she gets," Braxton says.

Farrah giggles. "Thanks for saving the rest of us from having to deal with a decaffeinated Tate."

Braxton's hand moves down to my waist, and the movement doesn't go unnoticed by me or my ex-boyfriend. The man beside me clears his throat, giving my hip a small squeeze, and turns to look down at me. "Well, I'd better get going. I just had to make sure you had everything you needed."

Farrah waves a dismissive hand and says, "Don't be silly, you should stay!"

All three of us look at her like she's miraculously grown a second head. What did she just say?

"I don't think this is a good idea." Braxton chuckles nervously. "I don't want to be in the way of your big day."

"Nonsense. You're part of our lives, too. And that's what this weekend is about, right?" She shrugs, like this is completely normal, but not a single second in the last five minutes has been *normal*. "Unfortunately, or I guess fortunately for you, we've sold out the whole resort. So, you'll have to share a room."

Shit.

Shit, shit, shit, shit, shit.

"Farrah, this isn't necessary. We are completely happy to go our separate ways for a few days. It's really not a big deal."

"Oh, please. I refuse to be the reason you don't get to spend Christmas with your *new* boyfriend. I was starting to think you'd never find someone after Colin."

Colin Montgomery, better known to fans as *Colin Ryker*, is another wrestler at EWE. We dated for almost two years before we broke up five months ago. The breakup wasn't something I was losing sleep over, but I wasn't looking to jump into bed with the next available guy I met, either.

My mouth twitches and I force it upward into a tight smile, glaring at my "boyfriend." "I'm sure I can convince the hotel to bring a rollaway bed or something."

"Oh, c'mon, Tate. You don't have to pretend like you're not sleeping together for our sakes." Farrah winks at me, and my mouth falls open.

This is not how I pictured any of this going, not that I pictured it at all. That's a lie. Seeing Braxton again was one of the only things on my mind on my drive up from Salt Lake City. I couldn't stop thinking about how good it felt to be with him again, how easily we fell into such a comfortable space with each other, and how the moment I left, there was an ache in my chest begging to be soothed by his presence. But this certainly is not how I envisioned that happening...

Braxton clears his throat, drawing my attention back to the version of him standing in front of me, not just the one in my head. "Well, then, we'd better get going. Looks like I need to make a run to get my stuff."

"You'd better hurry. I expect to see you at dinner," Farrah says. She curls into her fiancé's side, but he barely notices.

Micah's glare intensifies, boring into the man next to me, and honestly, I find his reaction to be a little...excessive. Sure, he and Braxton aren't friends anymore, but he seems more irritated than he should be. And it only makes me wonder if what Braxton told me is true. Maybe Micah's reaction to seeing him isn't out of anger at all, but fear. Fear that if Braxton and I are dating, there's a good chance he told me about Micah coming to him for money. And that means I *know*.

Just as the thought crosses my mind, Micah's gaze meets mine. The look in his eyes confirms everything I need to know. It reminds me of a wild animal narrowly escaping a trap. He's scared, confused, and he doesn't know what we're going to do with this information. And frankly, neither do I.

"Are you fucking kidding me?" I ask the moment the door to my room closes. I drop his hand but don't take the two steps backward I should take to put space between us. "What in the hell, Braxton? We haven't talked in years, and now all of a sudden, we're *dating*?"

"What did you want me to do?" The neutral expression on his face pisses me off.

"Anything would have been better than that!"

Braxton chuckles, shaking his head. "Look, I'm sorry. I didn't mean to make this worse, but you know as well as I do, Farrah would've had a lot more questions if we said anything else."

I cross my arms over my chest, standing ten toes down as I glare up at him. "You realize what you've done, don't you?"

"Please enlighten me, *Princess*."

My glare narrows even further when he references my in-ring persona.

"You've just put a fucking target on our backs, Bray. Micah *knows*. He knows that I know. He knows if we're 'dating,' you would've told me about him coming to you. And he's—"

"Tay," Braxton interrupts, taking hold of my hands to stop me from pacing. When did I start pacing? His thumbs begin to move in slow strokes across my skin. "Breathe. Micah doesn't *know* anything. He only thinks he knows something, and as long as you play this right, he doesn't have to know anything until you say something to Farrah."

"I can't—"

"You have to, Tate. If you were in her shoes, wouldn't you want her to tell you?"

I swallow back the rest of my rebuttal. He's right, but I also can't say with almost one-hundred percent confidence that Farrah would tell me if she knew something. "So, I tell her and...what? You swoop in to comfort her and be her knight in shining armor?"

"No." His answer is firm, like a line drawn in concrete, not sand. "No, I can promise you getting back together with Farrah Frost is the last thing on my list of things to do. Had you not left your purse this morning, I would be as far away from Snowhaven Springs as possible to avoid all of"— Braxton's hand gesture is a vague circle—"this."

"If not that, then why are you so worried if she knows or not?"

"Because it's the right thing to do, Tate." He sighs, carding a hand through his hair and tugging on the ends. "You know as well as I do what this issue can do to a relationship. While I may not like how she and Micah got together, I don't wish her any harm. I only want her to know what she's getting into, to have all the information before she ties herself to that fucker for the rest of her life. Because if I'm being honest, losing Farrah was the best thing that happened to me." His gaze lifts from the floor, and with those final ten words, the room feels so much smaller than it did seconds ago. The words feel heavy, like he's trying to say something without saying it, and all I can do is stare. In the blink of an eye, I watch a shift happen inside him, and then he breathes out a heavy exhale. "You said it yourself; you never told her. Who's to say he did?"

I'm still not past his admission from moments ago. What does he mean that losing her was the best thing to happen to him? I thought he loved her. I thought he was happy with her? What...changed?

I groan, covering my face with my hands, and fall to the edge of the bed. This is all so much. Too much. All I wanted was to come here, get through the next few days without incident—but with a good amount of wine—and go home to be with my family for the rest of my time off.

"Look, I'm gonna go," Braxton says, and I look up from my hands. "You can tell them I had something come up for work—"

"Oh, no," I say, jumping from the bed. "No, no, no. You're not getting out of this so easily. You're stuck with me, mister."

"I don't think having me around here is a good idea."

"Well, neither do I, but you got us into this fucking mess, and now you're going to see it through." What am I saying? I sound insane. And from the way his brow arches a little higher with every word, I know he must be thinking the same. He can't leave, though, because if he disappears after that display downstairs, it's only going to make Farrah more suspicious. "For the next three days, you're going to be the best boyfriend anyone here has ever seen." Shit, did I say boyfriend? I meant fake boyfriend. "*Fake* boyfriend. You know what I mean!"

Braxton chuckles. "Are you sure about this?"

"I have a feeling I'm going to regret this, but...yes."

"Well, then I'm going to have to go grab some stuff from home."

"Can't Macie bring it to you?"

"Afraid I won't come back?" He laughs when I don't answer, stooping down in front of me and taking my hands in his. "You said it yourself, *honey*, you're stuck with me. I'm just going to run home, get some stuff together, and take care of a few things. I'll be back before dinner."

"Dinner is at eight."

"I'll be back by..." Braxton pulls back the sleeve of his sweater to glance at his watch. "7:50."

If he leaves, he has every opportunity not to come back, and if he doesn't come back, Farrah will have a lot more questions than she already does. But this is Braxton...He wouldn't do that. Right?

"If you don't—"

"I'll be right back, I promise."

5

The weight of Braxton's hand on my back is more comfortable than it should be, making me feel safe and secure from the prying eyes behind us. The others decided to linger in the private dining room, carrying on the same conversations we'd been listening to for the last two hours, but we'd had enough. I can only listen to Maggie Frost tell the same stories about Farrah so many times in one lifetime. Dinner was uneventful—thank God—minus the grilling we received from the mothers of the bride and groom halfway through. I was surprised they even lasted that long.

"You know," Braxton whispers, pulling me in close once our steps slow outside the restaurant. The others are still filing out of the private dining room at the other end, but it won't be long before they've joined us. "For a man who's supposed to be getting married in a few days, Micah sure has spent an awful lot of time admiring someone other than his future wife tonight."

"What?" I practically snort, taking a step back.

Braxton pulls me back into his embrace. "Don't act like

you haven't noticed, Tay. Whenever Micah isn't busy mentally stabbing me, he's been staring at you like he remembers what you look like underneath that dress."

I scoff—he's being ridiculous—but Braxton refuses to let go when I try to pull away.

"I wonder what Farrah would think if she knew what her soon-to-be husband has been thinking...Then again, can't say I blame him."

I gasp. Surely, he didn't just...No, I must be hearing things. This thing between us isn't real. Why would he say something like that?

Braxton leans in closer than he was moments ago. So close, I can see where gold melts away into the prettiest hazel green I've ever seen. So close, I'm certain he's going to kiss me. "Smile, Pretty Girl."

And I do.

The nickname, accompanied by his own smile, makes my insides melt and my brain a little fuzzy. He's never called me that before...not that I can ever recall.

"Don't look now, but I think we're making him jealous," he whispers.

I laugh. "Oh, now I know you're lying."

"Braxton," I hear Micah say, and my stomach clenches. Maybe Braxton wasn't lying. Pulling away from our embrace, I find the groom standing not even ten feet from us. His arms are crossed tightly over his chest and daggers are in his eyes, pointing directly at the man beside me.

But Braxton still hasn't taken his eyes off me, the hint of a smirk on his lips. "Yes?"

"Join us, won't you?"

Finally, Braxton looks over at Micah. "I guess it depends on what you're inviting me to do."

"We're going to have a drink in the cigar lounge."

I can almost guarantee the invitation to join them was

not Micah's idea; it was probably Farrah's doing. Her reaction to this whole "dating" thing still bothers me. For years, she couldn't stand the idea of me and Braxton being anywhere near each other, but now you'd think she was rooting for us the whole time. Is this some sick game of *Gotcha*!? Or does she know we're only pretending, and she is hoping to catch us?

"Yeah, c'mon, Brax!" Micah's brother Reid says, joining us ahead of the group. He claps a hand down on Micah's shoulder, who tries to hide a small flinch under the weight. "We promise not to keep him too long, Tater Tot."

I roll my eyes. "How many times do I have to tell you to stop calling me that?" Every time he sees me, apparently, because every time I see the middle Evergreen child, he uses his favorite nickname without fail. I look over at Braxton and say, "You don't have to go."

"No, but I guess I should," he says. "You're joining the girls, anyway, aren't you?"

"Do I have a choice?"

Braxton chuckles. "No, I suppose not."

"You guys act like you're never going to see each other again. It's only going to be like an hour. Let's go," Micah says with a slight huff and stalks off.

Reid watches him before turning back to us with an eye roll. "Ignore him, he's been having a hard time at work, and he's letting it get the best of him."

Braxton brings the back of my hand to his lips, and heat creeps into my cheeks under his stare. "I'll see you later, Pretty Girl."

I watch him walk side-by-side with Reid, falling into an easy conversation like they used to, before the youngest Evergreen brother, Harrison, joins them and pulls Braxton into a one-armed embrace. The three men laugh, and I let out a breath I didn't realize I'd been holding. Maybe this won't be so bad, and it won't be as hard as I thought. At least Micah's brothers can still treat Braxton like a human being and not some intruder dressed in red-splattered grave clothes.

"He was never like that with me," a small voice says before an arm winds around my waist.

"What are you talking about?" I glance down at my best friend, her head now on my shoulder.

Farrah watches the same scene I'd just been admiring—a sad smile on her perfectly painted pink lips. With a sigh, she lifts her head. "Affectionate, passionate, whatever word you want to use...he was never like that with me."

"Again, what are you talking about? Yes, he was."

She scoffs. "Not like...*that*."

"Farrah—"

"It's okay, T," she says, and I internally cringe at the nickname. At least I hope it was internal. Call me crazy, but I've never liked the nicknames people have given me over the years. I prefer just Tate. "I'm not upset about it. It's just...I'm glad you guys finally admitted your feelings for each other."

"We didn't have feelings for each other. Braxton and I have always just been friends."

"Whatever you say, *Pretty Girl*." Farrah giggles to herself, shaking her head with a small smirk. She loops her arm through mine, dragging me toward the group of women awaiting us.

Shuffling into my room two hours later, I practically jump out of my skin when I turn the corner and hear the bathroom door pop open, the wood swollen from the moist air on the other side. I wasn't expecting Braxton to be back already. I half expected the boys to be out until one or two in the morning and figured the other Evergreen brothers would have convinced him to stay. Lifting my gaze, the words get stuck in my throat when I see him walk out dressed in only a pair of sweats low on his hips. Lean, well-defined muscles in his chest, shoulders, and arms with a slight six-pack outline in his lower abdomen make it hard to look away. Braxton isn't exceptionally chiseled, not like the men I spend the majority of my time with, and something about that is...refreshing. He must work out, or maybe it's just from all these years working construction; either way, I can't help but stare. Eyes roaming across his chest one more time, I notice the discolored line trailing his collarbone. That's...new.

"You okay?" Braxton asks, breaking the spell.

"Huh?" Ripping my gaze from his chest, I meet his knowing smirk, and the flames of a blush creep up my neck. "Oh, yeah. I'm just tired. It's been a long day. A long, weird day."

"You're telling me." He chuckles to himself, shaking his head as he turns away.

Without acknowledging him, I kick my heels off beneath my suitcase and toss the white gift box from Farrah on the dresser. She presented each of the bridesmaids with a small keepsake bracelet featuring three charms: a snowflake, a circle encasing our first initial, and another circle engraved with *Bride Tribe*. I shuffle through my clothes to find pajamas, deciding on sweats and a faded *"The Great" Fata* wrestling T-shirt. Glancing over my shoulder, I catch Braxton staring this time and immediately recognize the look in his eyes. It's the same one from earlier, before I was dragged away for champagne and dessert.

Braxton clears his throat. "How, uh...How was girl time?"

"Uneventful. You?"

"Typical Evergreen get-together. Take jabs at one another, add in a dash of ridicule, a pinch of hypocrisy, and there you have it." He shrugs, and I laugh. Sounds about right. "I left them when Reid suggested we head out to the strip club and casino."

Is he serious? Surely his brothers know about Micah's problem. Why would they suggest going to the casino?

"Did Micah go with them?" I ask.

"You think he's going to say no?" Braxton raises his brow. "That would mean admitting he has an issue, and we both know that's not going to happen."

"Shit." I sigh and tighten my grip on the clothes in my hands. I want to ask him why he didn't stay to make sure Micah doesn't do something stupid. If he's so worried about Farrah, wouldn't this be the perfect opportunity to prove to her what's been going on? Instead, I disappear into the bathroom to change.

He really is making this impossible—Micah, I mean. Braxton, too.

I have to tell Farrah. I have to. I have no choice, but damn, I do not want to have this conversation with her. This week is her wedding, it's supposed to be the best few days of her life, and bringing up Micah's issue isn't going to make it easy to keep the vision alive.

She's going to think you're jealous. She's going to think you want him back.

And that couldn't be further from the truth. My breakup with Micah had been a long time coming. The writing was on the wall, but we were comfortable—or I was. A breakup meant moving into uncharted territory, and I'd had enough of that with starting a new job on the other side of the country.

The process of getting ready for bed takes me nearly double the time it should, and even after I'm finished, I sit on the edge of the tub for a few more minutes, trying to organize my thoughts.

"What are you doing?" I ask when I walk out of the

bathroom and find Braxton straightening out a blanket on the floor.

"Well, some people would call it a pallet." He stands up, examining his work before looking up at me.

I scoff. "You've got to be kidding, Braxton. You are not sleeping on the damn floor."

"Are you suggesting we switch?"

"What? No." He cannot be that dense. "I'm suggesting you get your ass in this bed before I change my mind and *let* you sleep down there."

A soft rumble echoes in his chest, matching the smile on his lips. "You sure you're okay with this?"

"No," I say, climbing into bed and looking up at him. "But we're adults, and two consenting adults can share a bed. Besides, something tells me we're both going to need all the rest we can get to survive this week."

6

MONDAY, DECEMBER 23, 2019

Lifting the tray of coffees from the center console of my truck, I tuck the two pastry bags between them. One cup is her normal order: black with two ice cubes. The other is what used to be her favorite from The Fireplace, a local coffee shop down in the village: an apple cider chai latte. Whether she still likes it or not, I'm not sure; that's why I decided to get one of each. I can bear a little watered-down coffee if it means she gets to enjoy one of her favorite drinks, which she can only get at home.

I'd initially planned to grab something from the coffee shop at the resort, but the line was thirty people deep, and with as slow as the one barista was moving, I could make it down to the village and back before I'd even make it to the counter.

Call me selfish, but I found myself a little happy when I saw she'd forgotten her purse yesterday. It was refreshing to be around her without having to navigate the Farrah landmine— to feel like we could be ourselves again. Not to mention how we had fallen back into the same old easy rhythm we used to.

Was it a good idea to say we were dating? Probably not, but to say otherwise would've raised more questions.

I never anticipated Farrah inviting me to stay, though. I thought she would be more upset about the news. Any connection between me and Tate had been her biggest concern while we were dating, even though Tate was her best friend and would never do anything to hurt her. But if anything, Farrah seemed...relieved?

Tate looked like she was ready to strangle me the moment the words came out of my mouth, but after what I saw at dinner, I'm glad I'm here. Tate sat beside Farrah, listening to the conversation between the bride-to-be and two of the other bridesmaids, Bethany and Katie. She'd occasionally add something, but every time she did, I watched Katie roll her eyes, and Bethany completely ignore her. Hell, even Farrah barely acknowledged her. The whole thing felt...off. Like Tate was an outsider, intruding on their private conversation, but wasn't she supposed to be the maid of honor? Shouldn't they be happy she's here?

The whole night, Maggie Frost and Judy Evergreen kept a watchful eye on us, sharing glances when they thought no one was looking. One of those times, Tate caught Judy's glare. The Evergreen matriarch had never approved of Tate, but wasn't it time to let it go? Micah had moved on; obviously, we were at his *wedding* to another woman. A woman she did approve of. Unlike in the past, though, Tate didn't back down, and after what felt like a full five minutes, Judy dropped her gaze. And it wasn't even ten minutes later that we took a grilling from the two women.

"So, Tate..." Maggie had said.

I felt Tate's whole body tense under my touch, only relaxing slightly when I gave her thigh a gentle squeeze. Farrah's mother is intense; that's the nicest way I can describe her without sounding like an asshole.

"How long have you and"—Maggie's gaze flickered to me—"Braxton been dating? Farrah tells us she's just found out today."

Tate cleared her throat, sitting a little taller in her seat. "Not long, it actually came as a bit of a surprise."

"Oh, really? I have to admit, I wasn't shocked when she told us. You two have always seemed very...close."

Was she implying something was going on between us while we were dating their children? *Oh, that's fucking rich.*

"When did this reunion begin?" Judy asked.

Shit, we didn't talk about a backstory. We didn't have time.

Luckily, I already had an idea in mind. "I took my brother-in-law to a show in Salt Lake a few months ago," I said, and all eyes turned on me. "He's a big EWE fan, and I reached out to Tate to see if she'd be in town. Unfortunately, she wasn't there, but—"

"It was good to hear from him again," Tate said, a soft smile tugging the right side of her lips upward. She threaded her fingers through mine on top of her thigh.

"We started talking and just never stopped."

Judy huffed. "I can't say I'm surprised. I always thought you two would end up together."

"Oh, me too! Kind of like Farrah and Micah," Maggie said, and the two women fell into a fit of giggles.

Not long after, I pulled Tate to her feet as the others continued to carry on the same conversations we'd been listening to for hours. Our departure went mostly unnoticed, except for one person: Micah. I'd caught him staring at her throughout the evening—I lost count after the twenty-fifth time—and every time he'd look away, pretending like he had only been scanning the room, which was probably for the best. The last thing I'm sure he wanted was to be caught by Farrah staring at her best friend the same way he used to look at Farrah before they started dating.

Not that I could blame him. Tate looked absolutely delectable last night. The black material of her dress clung to her curves, the long sleeves and almost calf-length hem creating a modest and elegant appearance. But the open back caught my attention the moment I saw her. I couldn't help but stop and stare, admiring her as she walked down the hallway, hips swaying in a natural, unforced motion. I silently thanked God, because for the next three days, that woman was all *mine*. For the next three days, I wouldn't have to keep my hands or thoughts to myself.

"Braxton, hey!" A cheery voice breaks through my thoughts. *Farrah*. She waves at me as I reach the porte cochere of the resort.

"Mornin', Farrah," I say, offering her a small smile. I try to move to the side of her, but she blocks my path.

"The Fireplace?" she asks, glancing down at the tray in my hands. "You know there's coffee here, right?"

I shrug. "Tay doesn't make it home often. I wanted to make sure she gets to enjoy some of her favorite things while she's here."

Farrah's mouth twitches slightly. "That's...sweet."

"Yeah, well, if you'll excuse me."

"I'm glad you guys finally admitted your feelings for each other." Her words stop me. "It was always so obvious you liked each other."

I'm going to regret this, but... "What are you talking about?"

"Oh, c'mon, Braxton. Don't be coy. You only dated me because she wasn't available."

"You cannot be serious, Farrah. I dated you because I wanted to. I said yes when you asked me out the first time because I wanted to. It had nothing to do with—"

"So, it wasn't to make Tate jealous?"

"No. Despite what you think—what you've always

thought—some of us can be in a relationship without wishing it was someone else." That shuts her up. "Look, I don't have time for this. Tate is going to be awake soon, and—"

"Do you ever think about it?"

"Think about what?" The last word comes out in a slight huff.

Farrah smiles a soft, almost sad smile. "Us. If I had stayed."

She cannot be serious.

"No, Farrah," I say, shaking my head. "Now, if you'll excuse me, my *girlfriend* is probably wondering where I am." I don't wait for her reply as I walk through the lobby doors and straight to the elevators.

When I walk inside our room, the bed is empty with covers strewn haphazardly to the side as a fire roars in the stone fireplace across the foot of the bed. The curtains have been pulled, allowing the morning light to stream in as it glistens off the fresh snow that fell overnight. The whole scene looks cozy, the perfect setting for a day in bed together.

"One of those for me?" Tate asks, stepping through the sliding door from the balcony. What was she doing out there in nothing but her pajamas? It's freezing. "I was beginning to wonder if you'd left without saying goodbye."

"I think you're confusing me with the man getting married in a few days." I pluck the chai from its holder and pass it to her, along with one of the pastry bags containing a homemade cinnamon Pop-Tart.

Her eyes light up in recognition the moment the drink touches her tongue. "Apple cider chai. You remembered that, too?"

When I pulled into The Fireplace this morning, I immediately thought about the time when I'd met up with Micah and Tate in town a few years ago, and she'd asked him to pick up a drink while she ran inside her parents' antique store.

The barista, Chloe, greeted me and Micah from behind the counter with a cheery smile and wave. "Hey guys! What can I get you?"

Micah hesitated, eyes widening as he looked up at the chalkboard menu. They scanned over the curvy letters detailing each drink, but the longer he stood there, the more frantic they searched. *Does he not know what she drinks?*

"Shit," Micah mumbled under his breath.

"Dude, how do you not know what your girlfriend drinks? She used to come here almost every day before she moved."

"I'm sorry, I've never paid attention to every order she's ever placed," he said and huffed, crossing his arms.

I shared a look with Chloe, and her smile fell slightly. She recomposed herself quickly, though, maintaining the cheery attitude expected of employees at the café. "This is for Tate? She usually gets the apple cider chai."

"Let's do the candy cane, mix it up a bit," he said, completely ignoring the answer to his predicament Chloe had just offered.

Once more, Chloe glanced my way. *Is he serious?*

I sighed, shaking my head as I watched him hand over a five-dollar bill and walk away.

When we met up with Tate to deliver her coffee, the disappointment immediately settled in her features when she took the first sip. It wasn't the drink she'd wanted, nor expected, but without missing a beat, she praised her boyfriend anyway for "remembering" her order. Micah smiled and said, "How could I forget?"

Tate closed her eyes, sighing, and when they reopened, she met my stare. I offered her a brief smile, but she didn't return it. Instead, she turned on her heel and followed Micah farther into the store.

That trip had been one of the few she'd managed during her time in NextGen, the developmental program for EWE.

Micah and Tate had been dating for over three years by then, and Farrah and I had been together for almost two. That day was the first time Tate and I had been around each other without Farrah in a long time, and it would be the last until now.

Looking at her now, I can't help but smile with a small shrug. "You only used to get one every day."

Tate doesn't say anything else, taking another long sip of the warm beverage as she strolls back to the bed.

"What are my duties for the day?" I ask.

With another sip of her drink, I know the moment the liquid touches her tongue when her eyes flutter closed and a soft hum follows. "We have brunch. Then the girls have a fitting around one."

"What time is brunch?"

"Ten."

"I'm surprised she isn't requesting your presence before then," I say as she pulls the covers back over her legs.

Tate yawns, settling back against the pillows and pulling out the pastry. "She did."

"You know it's almost nine, right?" I ask, glancing at the clock on the nightstand.

"Yep," she says behind another sip of her chai.

"Well, when she comes breaking down the door, you don't get to blame your tardiness on me this time."

"Oh, c'mon. Don't you want to see Micah's head explode?" She scoffs, picking a piece off the pastry and popping it in her mouth. "He probably thinks this is confirmation we were fucking around behind his back the whole time."

"As much as I'd like to see him get a taste of his own medicine, that's not why I'm here."

Her eyes slowly narrow when she looks up from her lap. She's still trying to figure out exactly why I'm here—the real reason I want Farrah to know the truth about Micah.

But it's not what she thinks.

I don't want Farrah back. Hell, she can go through with the marriage even after she knows the truth, for all I care, but I think she deserves to know what she's getting into. If the roles were reversed, I hope someone would do the same for me. I'd want to know if my bride-to-be was gambling away not just our wedding fund, but our life savings. And trust me, if Micah stooped as low as to come to me for money, I know things are getting dire.

"I should probably get ready," Tate says, finally looking away. Popping the final piece of Pop-Tart into her mouth, she stretches her arms high above her head, bending from side to side, before dragging herself back out of bed.

"Braxton," Judy calls out from behind me, catching up before I can leave the restaurant. I'd almost forgotten how cumbersome it is to eat a meal with the Evergreens and Frosts, but especially the Evergreens. "Do you have a moment?"

I stare down at the woman who welcomed me into her home many times over the years, the same one who turned on me as soon as I tried to tell her about her son's problem.

"Sure, Judy."

She leads me out of the restaurant and a few steps farther down the hall, where the rest of the group has started to gather. The girls have a final dress fitting in less than an hour, and the guys are hitting the slopes—an activity I won't be joining them on. I have other things lined up that I can't forgo just because I'm now expected to at this wedding.

"I don't want you to take this the wrong way, dear, but are you sure you want to join us this week?" Judy asks, and if it were any other person, one might think she was being considerate of my feelings, but I know better.

"It's good to see you, too, Judy."

"Oh, you know that's not what I meant." An awkward laugh and a small wave accompany her words. "I just meant, I didn't know you and Micah were speaking again. We didn't plan for you to be here."

I'm sure you didn't.

"Occasionally," I say.

Her wary gaze moves to my side, where I know Tate has just appeared with Farrah. Judy hums softly to herself, turning back to me. "And you're dating Taylor now."

Taylor. Tate's government name. She's always hated how Micah's mom uses it instead of the name she's gone by her whole life.

"*Tate* and I have reconnected recently, yes."

"That's nice," she says with a tight smile, and I can only offer the same. "I always liked her."

No, you didn't.

"You guys make a great pair. Funny how these things work out, isn't it? You and her, Farrah and Micah...You know, I always knew she and Micah were never going to work. He needed someone more reliable."

"Reliable?"

"No, that's not the word." Judy touches her finger to her chin, the perfectly shaped red nail a stark contrast to the paleness of her skin. "Someone...*there*. Who isn't too busy flitting across the globe with a bunch of half-naked men instead of standing by her soon-to-be husband's side."

"You know she makes at least triple the amount of money Farrah does, right? Hell, she probably makes more than Micah does. She's one of the top women's wrestlers in the company and by proxy in the world. She was named one of Sports Illustrated's top women athletes last year."

"Oh, sweetie, you don't believe that, right? EEW, or whatever it's called, is all staged. They're not real athletes. She paid for those awards."

I take a deep breath, rolling my bottom lip between my teeth, and try to think of a better response than the one I want to say. I'm not going to win this fight, and it's not worth even trying. These people made up their minds about Tate and her livelihood a long time ago.

"Regardless, I think it all worked out for the best! Micah has Farrah now, someone who genuinely cares about him and his needs."

"You know what? You're right, Judy. Because now Tate has someone who genuinely cares about *her* and her passion. Someone who isn't ashamed of her, who's proud to show her off and bring her home to his family. Someone who isn't worried about where the next hit is coming from."

Judy gasps. Her eyes widen, and her mouth opens and closes at least three times.

Shit, I shouldn't have said that.

"Judy!" Farrah's voice rings out, but neither of us acknowledges it. Not until she yells out again. "Are you coming with us? We're on our way to the final dress fitting."

Mrs. Evergreen clears her throat and straightens out the bodice of her dress, wiping her hands on the fabric, no doubt suddenly wet with perspiration from the unexpected blow I delivered. "Y-yes. Yes! You know I wouldn't miss it, Farrah." She glances at me one more time. "It was good to see you, Braxton."

"You too, Judy."

"What was that about?" Tate asks when she greets me after passing Judy, who doesn't even so much as look up at her.

"Oh, nothing. Just a little chat."

Her eyes narrow, and I watch her tongue poke into the

side of her cheek. She doesn't believe me, but I'm not going to tell her I almost gave myself away to Micah's mom.

"Aren't you supposed to be leaving?" I ask, nodding at the group of women who've started walking down the hall.

"Yes, and you're not invited, in case you were wondering."

"Damn, I always wanted to know what I'd look like in one of those dresses you ladies wear." A dramatic, heavy sigh. "Always the groomsman, never the bridesmaid."

Tate rolls her eyes but doesn't fight a smile.

Movement catches my attention behind her, and I glance over her to see Micah glaring at us. His arms are crossed tightly, feet spread hip-width apart, chest puffed out...

Wrapping my arm around Tate's waist, I hear the soft exhale of breath as I pull her close. There's a small hint of citrus on her breath from the mimosa she had with her breakfast. Her hands land firmly on my chest, and her gaze slowly travels up until it meets mine.

"Guess I'll just have to settle for getting to stare at you instead," I say, looking down at the limited space between our bodies. "Imagining what it must be like to touch you in all the same places as that silky fabric..." I lean my forehead against hers, hearing the soft intake of breath. "Before I cart you off upstairs and take it off to feel your skin on mine."

"Bray—"

"Don't," I say, tightening my hold on her when she tries to pull away. I lean in a little closer to whisper in her ear, "They're listening."

She swallows so hard I can hear it travel back down her throat, but she does as she's told.

I press a kiss to her temple before I finally take a step back. "I'll be here when you get back."

Tate breathes out before straightening her shoulders and meeting my stare. "T-try not to get into any trouble. Or cause any."

I lift my right hand in the air, pressing my pinky down with my thumb, leaving the three middle fingers lifted. "Scout's honor."

She rolls her eyes with a smirk, turning on her heel to leave, but jumps back when she practically runs into Farrah. When the hell did she get there? Tate clutches her chest. "Jeez, Farrah! You almost gave me a heart attack."

My ex-girlfriend stands with a beaming smile, looking between the two of us. "You guys are so cute. I was just coming to invite Braxton to join the guys up on the slopes. I wasn't sure if Micah offered, and I wouldn't want you to feel left out while I keep Tate busy."

"Thanks, Farrah, but I'm good here. I have some work stuff I need to take care of."

"It's always work with you," she says, rolling her eyes. "You're almost as bad as Mick. He's been working so much lately, I feel like I never see him."

As much as I want to look at Tate, I know better.

"Well, you go have fun *working*. We're going to have some girl time." Farrah loops her arm through Tate's, dragging her down the hallway.

7

Farrah and I walk arm in arm through the newest boutique in Snowhaven Springs. This is the first time we've been alone, and the only thing I can think about is how this is the perfect opportunity to ask her about Micah. While we were at the dress shop, she was constantly surrounded by either the seamstresses or her mother, leaving me alone with Judy— who had been acting even more distant than normal since her "chat" with Braxton earlier— and the other bridesmaids. If you didn't know them, you'd probably think Katie, Morgan, and Bethany were all the same person: skinny, blonde, and usually dressed in some variation of pink. I stood out among them with my dark, dirty blonde hair that looked more like a light shade of brown. Not to mention, you wouldn't catch me dead in anything they have on. Their wardrobe always has a way of making mine look like it belongs to a hormonal teenager on the brink of puberty who recently discovered alternative dad rock.

But now...I have Farrah all to myself, at least for a few more minutes before the others come looking for us. This might be my only chance, but every time I start, I can't get the words to come out.

"Can I make a confession?" my best friend asks.

"Of course," I say, looking over at her.

Farrah sighs, patting my hand before giving it a gentle squeeze. She doesn't look at me, keeping her eyes on the collection of various trinkets lining the shelves, but when she finally does, I see the hesitation in her eyes. "I'm nervous."

"Nervous?" I chuckle. "I wasn't expecting that from you."

"Not in a bad way!" She backpedals. "I just...I don't know, it's hard to explain." Farrah pauses our steps, picking up one of the trinkets—a figurine decorated in an ornate white and blue pattern. She examines it before setting it back down on the shelf.

"What has you feeling this way?" I ask, and she shrugs. "C'mon, Fay. What's up?"

Farrah sighs again. "There's just so much pressure. I want everything to be perfect and—"

"Is it not?"

"It *is*. Everything is more than perfect, so I'm just waiting for the other shoe to drop."

If you only knew.

"Who says it will?" I ask, knowing I'm harboring my own confession, which happens to be the other shoe she's worried about.

"It's a week with both of our families and our closest friends in close quarters. I'm surprised someone hasn't been arrested for murder yet." A slight scoff before she laughs softly. "Not to mention, now Braxton is here—"

"Because *you* invited him."

Her brow cocks. "Would you rather I hadn't?"

"I didn't...That's not what I said," I say, ripping my gaze away from her prying one and forcing our steps to continue.

She stops walking again and refuses to let go when I try to

continue moving. "Why didn't you tell me, Tate?"

Because there's nothing to tell.

"I wouldn't have been mad," Farrah continues, but I can't contain my scoff. "What? I wasn't mad when I found out! I even invited him to stay so you'd have someone here with you."

"Oh, so the truth comes out," I say. "You only invited him because you feel bad I'm basically here alone at the wedding of my best friend and ex-boyfriend."

"That's not what I—I just meant..." Farrah groans, glaring playfully at me. "You're insufferable."

I laugh, and I don't know why I feel the need to apologize to her, especially when Braxton and I aren't really together, but I do. "I'm sorry for not telling you, Fay. We didn't want to cause you any more stress before the wedding than was necessary."

"At least someone doesn't."

Bingo.

This is the opening I've been waiting for. It feels like the universe is laying everything out on the table, and I wonder if Farrah really doesn't see something weird is—and has been—going on with Micah. Or maybe she refuses to. Since I met Braxton in the coffee shop, I've tried to recount my last conversations with my best friend. Had Farrah mentioned Micah working more than normal, or that he was making wedding planning harder than it needed to be? I can't remember. Actually, besides asking for my flight information and sending me an updated agenda, I can't remember the last time we spoke outside of her asking me for a loan.

"What's that supposed to mean?" I ask, and Farrah hesitates. "Is Micah giving you more issues?"

She's about to start backpedaling, but suddenly, we're interrupted by the obvious voice of her mother before she rushes to our side.

"Oh, Farrah! There you are," Maggie says, trying to maintain her composure, but it's quite obvious she's stressed. I'm not sure why. Farrah and I haven't left this aisle in over ten minutes. "We need to leave, or we'll be late to the cake shop."

"Shit, I almost forgot about." Farrah pinches the bridge of her nose before she turns to me. "We have to run by the bakery so I can test out the new flavor. Apparently, they can't get the citrus for the orange spice layer, and they can't find any cranberries."

"No cranberries? It's Christmas. There should be cranberries falling from the sky," I say, and my small laugh earns a glare from Maggie.

"That's what I said!" Farrah shakes her head, pulling her jacket over her shoulders. "But they were insistent cranberries would have to be from the can, and we all know those are not the same." Buttoning up her coat, she smooths out the fabric and looks up at me with a soft smile. "Guess I found the other shoe."

Unzipping my snow boots, I leave them by the door and shrug out of my coat to hang it in the closet. I pull my phone out of my purse and scroll through the notifications I had missed since we arrived at the cake shop over two hours ago. After listening to Farrah and the baker go back and forth, I didn't have it in me to so much as look at my phone after we loaded into the car to head back to the resort. There are a few notifications from the family group chat with my sister and our parents, two texts from Blair, one from another fellow wrestler, Cali Kennedy, and a handful of social media notifications. The only one I open is from Braxton; everything else will have to wait until after the holiday.

Braxton Powell

I'm back from work. Should
I meet you downstairs?

His text is from thirty minutes ago, and from the lack of his presence in the room, I think it's safe to assume he's already downstairs, waiting with the others. Normally, I would've gone straight to dinner the moment we arrived, but I need to change. I've felt constricted and stuffy in this sweater all day. If I'm going to have to sit through another two-and-a-half-hour meal, I don't want to be uncomfortable...or any more than I'm already going to be.

Pulling the sweater over my head, I breathe out in relief and prepare to answer his text when I run straight into the wall. Except this wall is different than any wall I've ever come across before. It has two hands and catches me when I stumble backward. *Holy shit, it's not a wall. It's him.* And not only is it him, but it's a very wet, very naked him. Okay, not completely naked. He's wearing a towel that is hanging dangerously low on his hips, and with one simple move would leave him completely bare.

Fuck me.

A bead of water runs down his chest, landing on the tip of my right-hand ring finger. My gaze drops to where my hands are currently splayed across his chest. From here, I can clearly see the scar along his collarbone. It's a little jagged, but it looks like it could be from where they stitched him back together. What is that from? I know he didn't have a scar here the last time I saw him.

Braxton clears his throat, drawing my eyes back up, and takes a small step back. He grips the towel where it's tucked in. "Sorry," he says, his voice a little deeper than normal, and he clears his throat again. "I, uh…I didn't know you were in here. I would've—"

"No, no," I say, and cross my arms over my chest, thankful I decided to put on a bra this morning. However, I'm not sure this posture is doing me any good; it only seems to make my breasts pop out further. "It's fine. I should've paid more attention. I thought you were downstairs."

"I had to go to a job site for a bit, so I needed a shower before dinner."

I nod, preventing my gaze from lingering on his naked body too long.

"You need the bathroom?" he asks, and I nod again. "All yours. I'll…I'll get dressed when you're done."

The next ten minutes might be the longest of my entire lifetime. Somehow, I went from one suffocating space to another, but this time for a completely different reason. We dance around each other, trying not to cross paths too many times, avoiding eye contact and conversation. I'm finally able to catch my breath when I walk out of the room, staying two steps ahead of him as I walk down the hallway. Not that it does much good, because the moment he steps into the elevator, the scent of his cologne hits me like a fucking wall, and the only thing I can think about is the way his body felt against mine.

I am so screwed.

I should say something—break the ice—because we cannot walk into the restaurant like this. Farrah would notice immediately, picking up on the tension.

I sneak a glance up at him from the other side of the elevator car and immediately wish I hadn't because he looks up from his feet at the same time. His hazel-green eyes swirl with what I can only assume are the same thoughts clouding my own right now. Without a word, his gaze falls back to the floor, and another stifling silence fills the space.

Just say something, I demand, but every time I look at him, all I can see is the image of him in just a towel. The way the water droplets trailed down his bare chest, glistening in the light, and the warmth of his taut skin beneath my fingertips. The weight of his touch on my waist, the gentle yet rough feel of his fingers against my skin.

How fucking long is this elevator ride?

I dig my nails into the palm of my hand and barely allow the doors to open before slinking out. I don't wait for him, walking straight to the restaurant. Fuck what Farrah might think. Unless she wants a show, I'm going to need a minute.

8

Braxton

"Thank God," Harrison says, meeting me at the door. "If I had to deal with all of them alone for one more minute, I think I'd implode."

Harrison Evergreen is the complete opposite of his brothers, or of his family, for that matter. The black sheep, if you will. Reid and Micah followed in their father's footsteps and went to law school. Micah became a litigation attorney, and Reid started in bankruptcy law before opening his own firm, which specializes in corporate law. But Harrison, the youngest of the Evergreens, never wanted to be a lawyer. For as long as I've known him, the kid was obsessed with food, and he went to culinary school, much to his parents' dismay. Needless to say, Reid is the pride and joy of the family, with Micah not far behind.

"We haven't had much time to talk," he says, guiding me toward the bar. I guess we aren't sitting down yet. "I can't even begin to tell you how happy I was to hear you were here. I thought I was going to have to suffer this weekend alone."

"You'd have Tate," I say.

"Yeah, right." Harrison rolls his eyes. "Farrah has held her hostage since she got here."

"Speaking of, where are they?"

I glance around the room, but don't see her anywhere. In fact, I haven't seen her since she bolted out of the elevator, and I was bum-rushed by a group trying to get on without giving me a chance to get off. I'd spent the entire elevator ride trying to think of a way to break the ice, but nothing felt right. I thought I had time to get dressed before she arrived, but that didn't exactly go as planned...

Feeling the warmth of her skin drew me in, and I'd lost every last one of my wits. Being so close to her, in such a compromising position...made all of those feelings from years ago come crashing back like a fucking tidal wave.

It was already hard enough sleeping in the same bed as her, but now I've seen her, held her, *touched* her in a way I've never been able to before...I don't know how I'm going to control myself. Just the image of her standing there, in only her bra, the sheer black lace leaving almost nothing to the imagination, is making it near impossible not to think about what it would be like to have her writhing beneath me.

For so long, I've kept myself in check around her. I had to. She was my best friend's girl. She was off-limits, and eventually, I guess, I convinced myself my feelings for her weren't real. They were just a case of good old-fashioned infatuation. Tate had never done anything to make me think she had feelings for me. Not to mention, she'd chosen Micah. From the first night we met, she'd chosen him. Decided he was the one she wanted. And despite Micah not always treating Tate the way I thought he should, I would have never done anything to betray my best friend or put her in that position. So, I chose to embrace a simple friendship with her. Well, as much of a friendship as we were allowed.

But now...Micah isn't a factor anymore. Neither is Farrah,

for that matter.

"Haven't seen 'em yet," Harrison says, shrugging as he holds up a finger to the bartender, asking for another round. "But I don't ask questions, I just show up."

"Smart man," I say, ordering a glass of whiskey myself.

"So," he begins, drawing out the word. "You and Tate, huh? Can't say I'm surprised."

Why does everyone keep saying that?

"Neither can I," Reid says, appearing at his brother's side. "Actually, I'm surprised it took this long. I thought you guys would have been tied at the hip the moment Farrah left."

Harrison leans back against the bar. "Yeah, why did it take so long?"

I look between them, a little stunned by their candor. "Well, I mean—"

"It's not like Mickey would've cared," Reid says. "I mean, he jumped on the Farrah train as soon as you guys broke up."

"Can you blame him?" Harrison laughs. "He'd been ready to climb aboard for a while. He wasn't taking any chances."

Reid joins his brother in another laugh, but I don't join them. In fact, I don't find anything about it comical. It wasn't like Farrah had given me much of a choice in our breakup, and it had taken less than two weeks from the first time we saw Micah after his sabbatical—as he'd called it that day in the store—for her to end things with me. Despite her denial, I knew it was because of him.

Micah and I had already been on thin ice. I hated the way he treated Tate in the end, but I had to keep my mouth shut or face the wrath of Farrah. So, I watched from afar as he continued to distance himself from his girlfriend, drag his feet whenever she'd ask him to do something, and bitch and moan when she had something to do for work instead of hopping on a plane to join him wherever the party took him for the weekend. The writing was on the wall, at least in my mind, but Tate held on. Longer than anyone else would have. So, why? I'd always been curious. Was it comfort? Fear of the unknown? Complacency? It was hard to tell when Farrah kept me so far out of the loop. Hell, I didn't even know about their breakup until two months later, when Micah mentioned it in passing at the poker table, only a week before he skipped town.

"So, Brax," Reid says, pulling me back to the conversation. "I hear you're doing pretty well for yourself. Got your own business and everything."

"I'm doin' alright."

"More than alright! Word is you got the bid for the renovations to the old resort out near Logan."

"We did," I say, and a small ounce of pride swells in my chest. "We start work in the new year."

"Glad to hear it. You know, we've missed seeing you at poker night. You should join us sometime."

"I'm not much of a gambler. Micah just needed backup, so he dragged me along."

"C'mon, Reid, you know Braxton doesn't have that kind of money to put on the line," Micah says, appearing practically out of thin air.

Speak of the fucking devil.

Harrison rolls his eyes hard enough for all three of us and swipes his fresh whiskey from bartender. "Neither do you, but you do it anyway."

Oh, shit.

"Shut up, Harry," Micah spits. "At least I make more than a line cook."

Low blow, but it's far from the truth. If I heard correctly last night, Harrison just got a new job as the head chef at a restaurant in downtown Chicago.

The brothers continue to go back and forth, trading blows, before their dad, Brad Evergreen, arrives and intervenes.

Through gritted teeth, he says, "Enough. I don't care who started it. Shut up. This is not the place for your bullshit."

As if on cue, the girls arrive, and Farrah beelines to her groom-to-be, clinging to him and draping his arm around her shoulders. Tate isn't far behind her, coming to stand beside me. *You're supposed to be a couple. Do something.* I slip my arm around her waist, half expecting her to push me away, but instead she moves in a little closer. Micah's gaze turns from the woman in his arms to the one in mine. He glides his eyes over her figure, pausing on her face briefly before sliding to the right to meet my unamused stare. His eyes narrow slightly, but I only offer him a tight-lipped smile.

"Tater Tot!" Reid shouts, and I try to hide my laugh.

"I told you to stop calling me that," Tate says with an eye roll.

"And when have I ever listened?"

"Never."

"Guess I can't start now, then!" Reid looks at me and shrugs with a half-cocked smile.

"Oh, Braxton," Farrah says, pulling not only mine, but Tate's attention toward her. "Just wait until you see your girlfriend in her dress."

"I take it the fitting went well?" I ask, looking down at Tate. She doesn't return the gesture, focusing on her nails now instead.

"She looked hot. You can totally tell she's been working out."

"Oh, trust me, I know," I say, giving Tate's hip a small squeeze. Finally, she looks up, her brown eyes wide. I smirk, letting my tongue poke out to wet my lips, and her chest heaves with a deep breath. "She looks damn good."

Micah huffs before he stalks off, mumbling under his breath, "Are we going to eat or what?"

9

"That's not fair!" Reid shouts from across the table. He points at me with the candy cane he's been sucking on for the last five minutes. "You literally have a *contractor* as your partner. Of course, your house is going to look the best."

I smile as Tate giggles into my side, her grip tightening around my arm, while Reid complains for the millionth time tonight. After dinner, the bridal party was invited to join the bride and groom in the bridal suite for a gingerbread house decorating contest. Upon our arrival, we were greeted by the sweet scent of freshly baked gingerbread laid out on the long dining room table, along with all the icing and decorations anyone could ask for.

"This is all you," Tate said when we sat down at the table. She leaned back in her chair, picking through the candy for what she could eat, and watched as I constructed a house that was starting to look more like a gingerbread mansion. It has two floors, two dormer windows, a chimney, a covered porch, and a front porch step...It isn't perfect by any means, but in comparison to the others...Well, let's just say, we'll definitely be taking home the prize.

"Who let them be on a team?" Reid resumes his griping.

Farrah rolls her eyes from the end of the table, where she adds more candy drops to the roof of her own house. She and Micah are supposed to be on a team, but he's nowhere to be seen. Am I surprised? Not in the slightest.

"Use the pieces of your house to build a gingerbread bridge and get over it, Reid," Harrison says, and snickers to himself as he lines the edges of his roof with icing.

The other bridesmaids crowd around a single house covered in all things pink. It looks like someone lathered it in a bottle of Pepto-Bismol, if you ask me, but as long as they're happy...that's all that matters, I guess.

From the corner of my eye, I notice Micah re-emerge from the hallway. He disappeared about twenty minutes ago, whispering something in Farrah's ear before he walked down the hallway, followed by the slam of the door. She rolled her eyes, only after he was gone, and only when she thought no one was looking. Where did he go? Beats me, but to be perfectly honest with you, I don't care.

He walks straight to the kitchenette and pours himself a fresh glass of whiskey. This has to be his sixth of the evening. He's been downing them a little harder than usual tonight.

Tate groans beside me, pulling my attention back to the table. She holds up a gingerbread tree that's been snapped in half. "This was the last one, too."

"Oh, good, we might actually have a chance!" Bethany says, her eyes lighting up.

"Yeah, right, Beth. Give it up, we all lost the moment he sat down," Katie says, never taking her eyes off their own house.

Tate stares down at the broken tree in her hands, and her face begins to morph into...Well, I'm not really sure what to call it. Sadness, maybe? Discomfort?

"You okay?" I ask.

She sighs, finally lifting her gaze to meet mine, and her body tenses, like she's bracing for the impact of my reaction. "I'm sorry."

I laugh, plucking the broken piece from her hand and taking a bite. "All good, Pretty Girl. Just means I get to snack on something."

"I'm sure she has something else you can snack on. Eh, Brax?" Reid says, wiggling his eyebrows.

Micah huffs from the kitchen. "Oh, for the love of God."

"Sorry, I guess I forgot we were in the middle of some weird partner swap thing."

The bridesmaids gasp, and Tate looks at me with wide eyes. Farrah quietly sighs, her shoulders barely raising an inch, as she tries to keep her focus on the house in front of her. But it's the most reaction she gives. Why is she acting like none of this bothers her? This is the complete opposite of how she reacted in the past.

Harrison starts to scold his older brother, but Micah beats him to it. "Shut the fuck up, Reid. Now is not the time for your bullshit. Can't you see it's upsetting Farrah?"

All eyes turn to her.

"Yeah, she's a real mess." Reid scoffs, rolling his eyes, and returns to placing gumdrops along his sidewalk.

"You know, Mick. He's not *wrong*," Harrison says.

"Here we go," Bethany sighs, speaking for all of us.

Micah glares at his youngest brother, but Harrison doesn't back down.

"Don't look at me like that," Harrison says. "Everyone is thinking it. Why not just say it? I mean, it's kinda funny when you think about it. Jason meant for Tate to meet Braxton that night, not you. But you, being you, decided that wasn't gonna fly. And now, here they are, together despite your best efforts."

Tate freezes beside me.

I turn my attention back to the tree in my hands, trying

to piece it together with only three pieces now, avoiding her stare.

"I don't know what you're talking about," Micah says through gritted teeth.

"Sure." Reid draws out the word under his breath.

Tate turns her attention away from me and looks at the youngest Evergreen. "Harry, what are you talking about?"

Harrison chuckles. "You mean you don't know?"

"Obviously, since I just asked."

"Jason was trying to set you up with Braxton, Tate, *not* Micah."

She doesn't say anything, but I feel her gaze shift to me again. I still refuse to look up, my hands fumbling with the icing and the tree pieces.

Harrison adds, "And Mickey couldn't stand the thought of Braxton getting the girl."

"That is not true," Micah spits out, the sound of his footsteps coming closer to the table.

I scoff, unable to contain myself.

"You have something to say?"

Finally, I look up and meet his cold stare, but don't say anything. Not for lack of trying. No, I have plenty to say, but this isn't the time or place.

Micah scoffs. "I didn't think so."

"Oh, shut up, Mick," Reid says, inciting another Evergreen brother bickering session.

When I glance to my side, I meet Tate's narrowed gaze. Questions continue to mount behind her eyes, rightfully so, but she won't ask them here, not in front of everyone. She'll wait until we're behind closed doors, or maybe not at all. I can't say for sure.

Did she really not know about Jason's intention? I guess it wouldn't have mattered, and it would have been hard to guess with the way Micah swooped in and stole the show. Not to mention, after Jason passed so suddenly a few months later, that night was the last thing any of us were talking about.

A few days before, Jason had mentioned his brother Judah might be bringing along a few of his co-workers from Wilder Wrestling Association, including a women's wrestler he'd told us about in the past. And I watched the little green monster crawl to perch on Micah's shoulder when Jason said he thought she and I should get to know each other. Micah let out a mixture of a scoff and a laugh, saying Jason only thought that because she was a wrestler and needed a "manly man" instead of someone with his head in a book. "Not at all," Jason said, laughing, and that sentiment would only become more obvious the more time Micah and Tate spent together. I hadn't had a chance to get a word in that night because when Jason and I walked in, Micah was already there.

My phone buzzes in my pocket, and I quickly pull it out, checking the name. "It's Macie, I'll be right back," I say, kissing Tate's temple without a second thought, and walk out the door to the balcony.

"Braxton, where are you?" my sister asks before I can even get a word in. "I've been trying to get in touch with you all day!"

"Sorry, I got a little...busy."

"Are you still coming with us to Mom and Dad's?"

"Shit." I sigh, rubbing the space between my brows. "No, Mace. I'm not gonna make it."

"You're not...What do you mean? You're the one who suggested it in the first place! What are you going to do for Christmas?"

"I, uh..." Fuck, how had I forgotten to tell her what happened? Is there really anything to tell, though? Tate and I aren't actually dating, and this is going to end as soon as Farrah and Micah say *I do* in less than forty-eight hours.

"Wait, hold on a second," Macie says. "You're not even

home! Why are you at the—Braxton, no. Please tell me you're not—"

"Are you tracking me?"

I knew I should've revoked her access to my location.

"Yes!" my sister snaps, ready to begin a verbal lashing. "And I want to know why you're at the fucking resort where Farrah and Micah are getting married in two days. You better not be—"

"Whatever you think it is…it's not. Trust me," I say, and switch hands, stuffing my now free one into my pocket to try and warm it up.

"Then please enlighten me. What are you doing there?"

"I don't have time for this, Macie."

"Well, you'd better make time, because…" My sister continues talking, but I'm only half listening when the door opens again, and Tate walks out.

What is she doing out here? She wraps her arms around herself against the cold, her long cardigan doing little to fight the single-digit temperatures. I motion for her to go back inside, but she doesn't budge. She averts her eyes, staring out over the banister toward the snow-covered forest in the distance.

"Hello, are you even listening to me?" Macie's voice brings me back to our phone call.

"Huh? Oh yeah, sorry, Mace. Look, it's complicated, but I'm not here to do *that*. Just trust me."

"Then why are you there?" It's quiet for a moment. "Wait… Did you call—"

Tate blinks, returning her gaze to mine. Without looking away, I say, "I'll explain everything when I see you Thursday."

Macie's voice rises an octave. "What does that mean?"

I feel like I'm dealing with a toddler whose answer is "Why?" to everything I say. "Macie, just let it go. I promise I will tell you everything when I see you."

Tate gently motions for the phone and slips it from my grasp, putting it up to her ear. "Hi, Mace." The other end goes silent. I count four Mississippis before Tate speaks again. "Yeah, it's me."

I hear a flurry of garbled questions from the other end, and I know I'll receive the same interrogation as soon as I get back on the phone. There's no way my sister will be able to wait until Thursday afternoon.

Tate laughs. "Yes, your brother is here with me. I'm sorry to steal him at the last minute during Christmas, but I, uh, I needed some help and—Oh, no. It's nothing like that." My sister probably asked if *she* is here to stop the wedding. "I just thought I could use the backup. He's in good hands." Tate's eyes widen before she breathes out a soft chuckle. "No, that's not...No, sorry, Macie. That's not it either." She brings her hand up to her mouth, chewing on her thumbnail—a nervous tick she's always had. What is Macie saying to her? "I know, Mace, I know. But that's not—"

The voice on the other line cuts her off, and Tate nods along, as if Macie were here and could see. Her brown eyes look almost black in the dim light when she looks at me. She glances away briefly before returning and holding my stare.

Her brow raises, and she asks, "Oh, really?" A small smirk tugs on the corner of her lips. "Well, I promise to return him in one piece on December 26th. Yeah, okay...Yeah, I'll tell him." Tate presses her thumb down on the red button at the bottom of the screen and hands my phone back over.

"Do I even want to know?" I ask.

"Probably not." Tate giggles, but her smile falters slightly. Most people probably wouldn't notice, but I can't help it. "You know Macie. Just making sure you're not doing anything that'll get you into trouble."

"She definitely thinks we're here to stop the wedding."

"I guarantee it's crossed the minds of everyone inside," she says, motioning over her shoulder toward the door.

"And yet, they let you stick around."

Tate shrugs. "My situation is a little different."

"What else did my sister say?" I ask, changing the subject.

"What?"

"She had you on the phone longer than just to ask what we're doing here. What else did she say?"

Tate swallows, her tongue poking out to wet her lips, more than likely dry from standing out here for so long, and she wraps her arms around her midsection against the cold again.

"Tay—"

"She asked if we were here...*together*."

Fuck, I was scared of that.

Macie has rarely brought up Tate, but a few months ago, I learned it wasn't for lack of thought. It was Beachbash this past August, and my brother-in-law had invited me over to watch it with him. Macie had kept to herself for most of the day. Actually, she disappeared as soon as I got there and returned a few hours later with a fresh manicure (and pedicure, I assumed) and an armload of groceries.

I walked into the kitchen to grab two beers, and her voice caught me off guard: "She looks good." She didn't look up from the fresh fruit plate she was preparing for my two-year-old niece, motioning to the television through the pass-through. It was only then that I realized who was on the screen: *Kerrigan Tate*.

Tate bounced off the top rope onto the canvas and lifted the EWE Women's Championship belt over her head. She smirked across the ring at her opponent, *Calla Lily*, who sneered in response. They had been in a bitter feud since *Lily* lost the title to *Kerrigan* at Wrestlefest in April.

"You talked to her?" Macie asked, popping a grape into her mouth before chopping another in half.

"Why are you asking?"

"I'm just curious. You guys used to be close."

"No," I corrected. "I used to be close to her boyfriend. She and I weren't—"

"Oh, whatever." Macie practically snorted. "You were friends, too. Before Farrah happened. Hell, you treated her better than her own damn boyfriend." I didn't have a response. What could I say? She wasn't wrong, but I'd never admitted it to anyone before. "I have to say, I was a little surprised you guys didn't start talking again after you and Farrah broke up."

"What are you talking about?"

My sister shrugged, eating another grape. "Like I said, you were friends, too."

"We've all moved on, Mace. Some people come into your life for a short time, and that's all they're meant for."

"So, given the chance, you'd just let her walk away again?"

"I didn't—" I pinched the bridge of my nose and sighed. "I didn't *let* her walk away."

"You didn't fight for her either."

"She wanted him, Macie."

"And what about what you want, Bray?" Macie slammed her hand down on the counter, finally turning to look up at me. Her blonde hair stuck out in different directions from her ponytail, and she had dark circles under her eyes. She'd been having a hard time adjusting to her return to work at the hospital after a long hiatus following Anya's birth.

"Everything okay in there?" my brother-in-law called over his shoulder.

"Yeah, we're good, Max," I said, and waited until I was sure his attention was fully back on the match before I continued. "She made her choice, Macie. She made it long before I ever had the chance to make mine."

"But Jason—"

I cut her off, shrugging. "It just wasn't meant to be."

"I don't believe you. You're telling me that if she walked through the door right now, you wouldn't take the opportunity?"

"I haven't talked to Tate in...hell, three, four years, maybe? If she walked in the door, I wouldn't even know her anymore."

"But what if you could see her again. Get to know her."

"You're being weird," I said, narrowing my gaze. Why was she bringing this up? We hadn't talked about Tate, Micah, or Farrah in a long time, but especially Tate. Not after the one time I drunkenly admitted I thought I was in love with her, a few months after she and Micah started dating. It was like Macie knew better than to bring it up...until now...seven years later. "Not to mention, I'm pretty sure she's dating one of the other wrestlers." *Colin Ryker*, I think. "Why are you bringing this up, Macie?"

She sighed. "I got Max tickets...to EWE, when they're in town next month."

"And...what about it? You want me to call Tate up and—"

"No!" Macie threw her hands up. Clearly, I wasn't understanding what she was trying to say. "No, of course not. I'm just thinking you could go with him." Her smile was pleading. "And if you're there, the seats are good seats, what if she sees you and you guys—"

"I think you've watched one too many chick flicks, Mace." I laughed, plucking a grape from the bag and popping it into my mouth. "The odds of seeing her, or her seeing me, are one in a million."

"There's always the wedding. She'll be in town for that."

I rolled my eyes. "And I won't be. I'm going to Mom and Dad's for Christmas."

"You didn't tell me that," Macie said, planting her hands on her hips.

"I'm telling you now."

"It would be nice not to have to play host this year..." She glanced around the house, gnawing on the corner of her lip. "Okay, count us in."

"I thought you'd fight me a little more."

Macie rolled her eyes and picked up the knife to return to her work, but paused. Looking back up at me, she asked, "Can I just say one more thing?"

"Mace—"

"I think you should reach out to her, Bray."

"If she had any interest in rekindling our friendship, she would've reached out after Farrah left."

"Don't you think she needs someone to talk to who isn't Farrah or Micah? Someone who understands what she's going through? Because I guarantee standing by while watching her best friend plan a wedding to her ex-boyfriend hasn't been easy."

"She's made her choice, Mace. Just like she did years ago," I said, plucking two beers from the fridge and walking out of the kitchen. I wasn't going to reach out to Tate when I could almost guarantee she'd moved on with her life, and I had, too...

"They're about to judge the gingerbread houses," Tate's voice rips through my thoughts, drawing me back to the present. The very cold present. I hadn't even realized that I zoned out. How long have we been standing here? Couldn't have been too long. But Tate smiles softly when I meet her eyes again. "We should probably get inside."

"Y-yeah, let's go," I say, stepping around her to pull open the door. "Why didn't you bring a jacket? You know it's like—"

"Hold on!" Farrah's outburst catches everyone off guard. She bounds out of the kitchenette with a glass of wine. "You, my friends, have been caught in what might be the most delightful holiday tradition."

"What is she talking about?" Tate whispers to me.

"Look up!" Farrah points above our heads.

We share a questioning glance before our gazes slowly inch upward. *You've got to be shitting me,* I think as a bundle of leafy green branches tied together with a red bow stares down at me.

"Farrah, you didn't," Tate mumbles.

"Go on, Braxy, kiss her!" Reid urges.

Finally, I draw my eyes away from the greenery and meet Tate's gaze again. Her face is pulled into a straight line, making it hard to read her.

"Don't be shy. Go for it!" Farrah says from behind her wine glass.

"Farrah," Tate warns.

Bethany scoffs. "You guys act like you've never kissed before."

The others laugh, and Tate bites down on her bottom lip, trying to withhold her own, but for a different reason. She looks back at me, and this time I see the nervousness behind her eyes. Are we really going to do this?

"It's okay," I mouth, and lean in close. Her breath hitches as I get closer, but just before our lips touch, I quickly maneuver to her cheek. The skin is still chilled from being outside, but she flushes under the contact. When I pull away, I lift the corner of my mouth in a quick smile, and she returns it.

"Oh, c'mon, man!" Harrison calls out from the couch. "What was that? *Kiss her!*"

This time, it's Tate who leans in and plants a quick peck on my lips. So fast, I don't have time to process what's happening until she's already pulled away. "There. Happy?"

"You've got to be kidding me," Farrah says, rolling her eyes. She looks me straight in the eye, ignoring Tate's ramblings about this being a silly, childish tradition. "Kiss her like you mean it, dammit."

Why is Farrah pushing this so hard? There's no reason for her to do this. Maybe it's guilt...Does she feel guilty for the way things ended on all sides, and now she's trying to make things right by pushing us together? The whole thing seems odd, considering the way she felt about any semblance of a friendship between me and Tate years ago.

Micah stands off to the side, nursing his drink. He's been silent throughout this whole ordeal, and I almost forgot he was here. His eyes are narrowed, but his stare isn't nearly as hard as it has been the past two days, not until he catches mine.

"Just do it," Tate whispers, bringing my attention back to her. "Just get it over with so they'll leave us alone."

I've never felt so much pressure when I'm about to kiss someone before, and her words aren't helping to relieve it. All eyes are on us—on me—and it's awkward, but the anxiety melts away when she looks up. A small smile appears in the corner of her mouth, but I don't return it.

I can't, or I might lose my resolve to do what she just commanded.

Instead, I suck in a deep breath and breathe it out slowly, reaching up to tuck a strand of dark blonde hair behind her ear. My fingers trail down her jaw, lifting her chin, and I cover her mouth with mine. The kiss is soft and hesitant, testing the waters, but then the switch flips. The same spark from the first time I felt her touch years ago appears. It spreads through my veins, setting my entire system on fire. Her fingers fist the front of my sweater to pull me closer, and it matches the desperation I feel creeping up inside me. The sweet taste of her, the way she fits against me—like she was made for me—and the soft moan for only me to hear...it's all too much. All I can think about is getting the fuck out of here.

Tate whimpers softly when I nibble on her bottom lip, pulling away. Her hand reaches to touch her lips, and when she looks up at me from under her lashes, I know I didn't imagine any of it. It was the same feeling I'd dampened down for so long because she was off-limits and I was sure it was only my longing to have what she and Micah had...But now, I know that wasn't true. That longing wasn't for what they had; it was for her. It had always been her.

I've never felt anything like this with anyone else, not even the woman on the other side of the room, who is currently staring at us like we've mortally wounded her. Her face is slightly contorted, trying to hide the thoughts racing through her mind, but unfortunately for her, I can see through the mask.

Why is she so upset? She's the one who initiated this whole thing, the one who hung the mistletoe in the first place.

"Now that is how you kiss a woman," Reid says, a smirk in his tone.

10

Braxton pulls away, nipping on my bottom lip, and a soft whine falls past my lips.

Nice self-control, Tate.

I can't help it. Everything inside of me calls out for him, begging him to come back and finish what he just started. My lips tingle beneath my fingertips, and an electric current flows through my veins with every beat of my heart.

Braxton's tongue pokes out to wet his lips before he glances down at my mouth. His eyes are filled with an aching need that mirrors my own. That kiss was the only answer I needed to the questions I had about Jason's true intentions. The questions about my feelings toward Braxton, the ones I've shoved aside for so long because I told myself he was Micah's best friend, and I was happy, and he was just being nice...

"Now that is how you kiss a woman," Reid chuckles, drawing my attention back to our current surroundings.

Shit.

Farrah clears her throat and excuses herself, setting the

glass of wine down on the table as she leaves with haste.

Double shit.

Braxton must read my mind because he smiles softly and reaches over to give my hand a soft squeeze with a nod.

Without a second thought, I follow the bride-to-be to the bedroom. My knocks go unanswered, and when I peek my head inside, the room is empty, but I hear her rummaging around inside the bathroom. A few moments pass before Farrah remerges, her face now makeup-free.

"Oh! Tate." Farrah plants a hand on her chest. "I didn't know you were in here."

"Are you sure you're okay with me and Braxton, Fay?" The words tumble out so fast, I don't have a chance to stop them. That isn't what I meant to say. I meant to ask if she was okay. But I guess my subconscious decided that wasn't good enough when deep down, I know the reason she ran off is because of what just transpired…even if she's the one who egged it on. But I also don't know why I care. Braxton and I aren't together…not really. Farrah doesn't know, though, and after that kiss…

Farrah plasters a wide smile on her lips, but it doesn't reach her eyes. "Of course, why would you ask a silly thing like that?"

"Because you just instigated an entire mistletoe kiss like we're in middle school, and then you ran away."

She scoffs. "I'm not jealous, if that's what you're implying."

Well, I wasn't until she said it.

"I didn't mean…" I sigh, crossing my arms. "I'm just giving you the chance to tell me how you feel." I'm giving her the opportunity she never gave me. There had been no room for discussion when it came to Farrah dating Micah.

"I'm happy for you, Tate," Farrah says, gingerly touching my hand. "But I guess…I guess seeing you guys out there, it hit me that he never really loved me."

I don't mean to laugh, but I can't help myself. "What are you talking about?"

Braxton treated her like royalty. He stuck by her through her master's program and the beginning of her PhD program. He supported her dreams and ambitions, never once doubting her. He even paid all the bills while they lived together so she could focus on school. Hell, he *proposed* to her a month before she dumped him for Micah. What did she mean he didn't love her?

"Not like that," she says, motioning toward the door. "He never kissed me the way he just kissed you."

"That's absurd. He loved you, Farrah. Ask anyone, they all saw it."

"Maybe, but it's not the same. Not the way he loves you."

My heart clenches at her words.

"It's okay. I guess I understand how you feel now," Farrah says, and lets her shoulders lift in a small shrug.

"You're the one who invited him to stay, Fay," I say.

She sighs. "I know."

"I can ask him to leave, if you want. I don't want to make things weird."

Farrah laughs. "I think we moved past weird a long time ago, don't you? I'm getting ready to marry your ex-boyfriend." She pulls me to sit on the bed beside her and rests her head on my shoulder. "I'm sorry for making *you* uncomfortable. I thought it would be a cute way to break the ice for you two."

That's one way to put it.

"Why didn't you tell me, Tate?" She sits back up, scooting away slightly so she can look me straight in the eye. However, there's no accusation in her tone, only pure curiosity.

"Tell you about what?" I ask dumbly.

"About you and Brax."

"Oh, I-I, uh..." I stumble on my words. What am I supposed to say? "It's still so new, Fay. I didn't want to say something when it may not go anywhere to begin with."

Farrah scoffs, waving her hand through the air. "You and Braxton have always been the better pairing. Of course, it'll go somewhere."

"We were never a pair."

"You were both completely blind to it. Micah noticed it, too. We all did."

I shake my head. "We were just friends because we had mutual friends."

"Whatever you say, *Pretty Girl*," she says with a smirk, knocking her shoulder gently into mine.

I roll my eyes but feel the blush creep up into my cheeks at the nickname. Trying to change the subject, I ask, "Did you know about the Jason stuff?"

"What?"

"What Harry said earlier…about Jason trying to set me up with Braxton years ago."

Farrah shrugs, but refuses to look at me, suddenly finding the invisible lint on her lap way more interesting. "No, I don't think so."

Lie.

"But I guess if it is true, Jason knew something we all didn't." She sighs and leans back on her hands to look up at the ceiling. After a quiet moment, she says, "Just don't break his heart like I did, okay? He's a good guy. He just…wasn't for me."

Neither is Micah, I want to say. Farrah could do so much better than Micah Evergreen.

"So, we're okay?" I ask. "And not just about the Braxton thing. I know I haven't been able to be here for all of this, and I feel terrible. I'm your maid of honor, but—"

"You're busy, Tate. I get it. You've been here when I needed it most, and that's the important thing."

"You've just seemed a little standoffish lately. More than

normal."

"It's not you," Farrah says, closing her eyes. "It's everything. I think this has been more stressful than getting a PhD." We both laugh before she sits back up, biting down on her bottom lip. "I'm so serious! I'd rather have to start all over than do this ever again. Micah has been the worst."

Shocker.

"You need to make him do something, Farrah."

"C'mon, Tate." Farrah scoffs, and I know the feeling all too well. "You know better. He'll just keep messing up whatever I ask him to do until I do it myself. Whenever I ask him for help, he tells me to decide or handle it. I mean, look, you've seen him the past two days…He's spent almost every minute on the damn slopes every day while I'm handling these last-minute details."

"Make him help you," I say again, emphasizing every word. "If you don't start now, he'll be like this for the rest of your marriage."

She shrugs. "It's not worth the argument."

"Fay—"

Farrah lifts her hand and plasters a smile on her face. "No, it's okay. I shouldn't have said anything. I'm just having a moment, that's all. Everything is great." My brow cocks higher with every word. I don't believe her, and she laughs. "I promise."

The real reason Braxton is here creeps to the forefront of my mind. This is the perfect time to say something to her, to try and bring Micah's problem to her attention. "Can I ask you something?" I ask.

"I guess," she answers, drawing out the last syllable.

"Are you…Are you sure this is what you want?"

Her smile falls slightly, and I'm surprised she doesn't force it back up. "Of course, I do. Why would you—"

"It's just…" I sigh. "You're right, I do know how Micah can

be, and I'm worried—"

"Farrah!" Micah's voice rings out as the door swings open. Speak of the fucking devil. "What is—Oh." His eyes are locked on me when I turn away from my best friend, and my gaze narrows slightly as his eyes roam freely over me. "Everything okay in here?"

"Oh, yes, dear. We're just taking a minute to catch up," Farrah says, taking my hand in hers. "What do you need, Mick?"

"Just wondering when you were going to get this show on the road. I'd like to be done with all this nonsense."

"Sweet words from the man I'm about to marry."

Micah rolls his eyes. "You know what I mean."

Farrah sighs one more time and rubs her hands on the tops of her thighs as she stands from the edge of the bed. Looking back at me, she says, "Well, c'mon. Let's go so you and Braxton can officially beat everyone."

"Actually, I think I'm gonna turn in for the night," I say, stretching as I stand.

"What? No! You have to at least stay for the vote."

"We're good, Fay. We'll see you in the morning."

"Eight o'clock sharp," she says, pointing her sharpened nail in my direction. We have a spa day before the big day, and to be quite honest, it's what I've been looking forward to most. Facials, massages, body wraps, and mani-pedis with a glass of champagne in hand? Say less.

"I'll be there," I say with a tired smile before turning to glare at Micah. He rolls his eyes, pushing by me before I can even make it out the door.

Braxton sits in one of the chairs in the living room across from Reid and Harrison on the couch. He laughs at something Harrison says before catching my eye. He must realize what I'm doing because he stands almost immediately and says, "G'night, gentlemen."

"You're joining us on the slopes tomorrow," Harrison calls after him, leaving no room for objection.

"We'll see."

"Oh, c'mon! It'll be fun," Reid adds.

Braxton's voice is much closer when he speaks this time, and he chuckles to himself. "I said we'll see."

The walk to our room is quick and quiet, thankfully, giving me a chance to try to come to terms with everything that's happened over the last few hours. I thought this was supposed to be a weekend of celebrating, not secret spilling. Not to mention, I'd been seconds away from telling Farrah about Micah. If he'd waited only a few more seconds, I could've gotten it out. It was the perfect time. We were alone, and she'd just admitted things weren't as perfect as she'd led everyone to believe. Not that I didn't already know, but with it out in the open, it couldn't have been a better time to bring up my reservations.

"You okay, Pretty Girl?" Braxton's warm voice draws me out of my thoughts. He kicks off his shoes when we walk inside our room but doesn't come any closer. His gray cable-knit sweater tugs tightly across his chest when he crosses his arms.

My voice is soft when I say, "I almost told Farrah."

"Almost?" His brow cocks. "Why didn't you?"

"I was about to, but then Micah walked in talking about the gingerbread houses."

"Runnin' a little short on time, here, Tay."

"I know!" I push a hand through my hair. "But what was I supposed to do? I can't bring it up in front of him. Do you want to see what World War III looks like? Because I guarantee that's where it'll start."

Braxton sighs and scrubs a hand down his face, leaning back against the dresser.

"What if she knows?" I ask, without being able to stop

myself. The thought has crossed my mind a few times this weekend. Don't ask me why, but it's something I've considered more than once. How could she *not* know?

"You think she does?" Braxton looks up to meet my gaze.

"I don't know what to think, honestly. But she has to know something is going on, right? Or at least suspect it."

"How long did it take you to find out?" Braxton asks.

"A while, but even after I found out, I didn't realize the severity of it...I tried to go to his parents about it, but they acted like I was overreacting," I say, and hear Braxton mumble something under his breath. It's not clear enough for me to make out, but I can assume it's not nice. "Brad bails him out; he always has. I still don't understand why Micah wouldn't go to him instead of you or me?"

"Maybe he finally cut him off. Don't give me that look. Everyone has their limits."

Not the Evergreens.

I sigh, already tired of this conversation. After the day we've had, the last thing I want to think about is Micah Evergreen. But if I end this conversation, it means moving on to the other elephant in the room: us, and what just happened under the mistletoe. Biting down on my bottom lip, I hold his gaze and see the recognition flash across his hazel eyes. "Bray, why didn't you tell me?"

"Tell you what?" he asks, and I scoff. Is he really going to make me say it?

"About Jason...and trying to set us up."

His body tenses. His arms coil a little tighter over his chest, but his eyes stay locked on me.

"You had every opportunity to say something, but you never did."

"I...I'm not..." Braxton sighs. "I'm not that kind of person, Tate. You were with Micah—you were happy with Micah—and he was my best friend...I wasn't going to get in the middle."

"But if you knew—"

"Would it have changed anything?" His question catches me off guard. "Because from where I stood, it would have only made me look like some pathetic loser, trying to call dibs. You made your choice, Tate, and I accepted that."

"A choice I didn't even know I was making. I wasn't given the option!"

"I wasn't going to put you in the middle of some bullshit game he was playing. Or put you further in the middle of it," he says. "There was no option, Tay. Not back then."

"And now?"

We both pause.

Where did that come from? Why did I say that? Do I want there to be an option now? And not just for show, not just for this week...Do I want it to be a real option?

I walk toward him, taking five cautious steps until I'm standing right in front of him. Braxton's brow furrows, but he doesn't back away. *He's never kissed me the way he kissed you,* is what Farrah said, and I think I almost believe her. Because I felt the spark when we kissed earlier. I felt something I've never felt with anyone before, and I know he felt it, too. There's no way he didn't.

"And now?" I repeat.

Braxton swallows hard. "Tay—"

"I want to try something, okay?" I ask. I wait for a brief moment before he slowly nods.

Closing the space between us, I hesitantly press my lips to his. Our lips brush, feeling almost like the whisper of the wind blowing gently on an autumn day. But soon, his patience wears thin, and Braxton completely closes the gap between us. His mouth claims mine in a hard, dominating kiss. This is different. This isn't for show under the mistletoe. It's not trying to prove anything to the rest of the group, to show we're not a threat to the wedding. This is real. Raw.

I drape my arms around his neck, tightening my hold on him as our mouths move together, tongues caught in a desperate embrace. His hands trail down my sides, touching, squeezing, discovering, before they reach down and cup my ass. Braxton lifts me off my feet, setting me on top of the dresser before standing between my legs. He towers over me, and from this angle, he can devour me completely...and I let him. I let him in, let him explore and taste, and I do the same to him. Our bodies move in sync, almost like this is exactly what they've been waiting for.

Dark, wanton eyes stare back at me when we part, heavy breaths filling the space between us.

Shit, that's what I've been missing?

"Bray—"

Braxton chuckles softly, adjusting his stance slightly. "Careful, Pretty Girl. You're about to cross into dangerous territory." The struggle to restrain himself is visible in his movements and across his face. Clearing his throat, he steps away, and I immediately feel cold without him there. "And as much as I want this...Want to have you, to taste you, and feel you come undone beneath me..." His admission makes my breath catch in my throat. His eyes bore into mine. "Not here. Not like this. Not because of some silly holiday tradition. Or because you're questioning the past...I only want this—us—if and when you're sure it's what you want."

His lips lift into a slight smile before he reaches out to catch my hand and bring my knuckles to his lips. With a deep breath, he drops my hand and turns on his heel, leaving me dazed and confused.

11

Tate

TUESDAY, DECEMBER 24, 2019

The last thing I remember from last night is trying to force my eyes back open as I lay in bed, waiting for Braxton to come back from wherever the hell he disappeared to. However, the confining weight on my midsection tells me I'm no longer alone in bed. His warmth is a heavy presence against my back, and blinking my eyes open, I check the alarm clock on the nightstand. I still have five minutes before I need to get up...and instead of forcing myself out of bed on the count of three, I slowly roll onto my back and face him.

He breathes in deeply, then blows it out, and his hazel eyes blink open. The small rim of gold around his pupils is prevalent in the morning light streaming through the crack in the curtains. Braxton groans softly, reaching up to rub his eyes with his thumb and forefinger before he meets my stare. We lie like that for a moment, just staring at each other, until the corner of his mouth quirks. "You're going to be late if you don't get a move on," he says, voice still thick with sleep.

"Probably," I say, still not moving.

"She's going to kill you, and then me."

"It's possible."

A beat of silence follows, and the moment feels too intimate for two people who are only pretending to date. Not to mention, we haven't been "friends" for years. But it feels... right. Waking up next to him—being around him—feels normal, even after all these years.

His eyes quickly flash down to my lips before returning to mine, and a pit forms in my stomach, one of longing and desire for the man beside me.

"W-where did you go last night?" I ask.

"For a walk," he says before clearing his throat. "I needed to get out of here before I did something we'd both regret."

"You'd regret it?"

A small chuckle before his tongue skates across his teeth. "No, but I know you would."

"No, I wouldn't," I say, and I mean it.

Braxton's face falls slightly, taking in what I just said, and for the second time this morning, his eyes drop to my mouth. This time, they linger there as I move closer to him. Everything I had planned to say last night goes out the window as I inhale the intoxicating scent of him and feel the warmth of his skin on mine. I lean in closer, letting my lips brush over his.

"Tay," he practically begs. His hands fall to my hips, but whether he's going to push me away or pull me closer, I can't tell.

"Did you mean it?" I ask.

"What?"

"You want this? Want me?"

Braxton doesn't answer, but I can hear the thick swallow in his throat, feel the way his mouth purses around the sensation. He interrupts me when I try to push, "You don't want this, Tate."

"Says who?" I pull back to meet his gaze again, and he pulls away even farther.

Braxton falls onto his back and stares up at the ceiling with a soft laugh. "You're just caught up in everything going on. When this is all over, when we leave here, we'll go back to the way things have always been."

"That's not true," I say, sitting up. "You don't know what I want, Braxton."

He mirrors me, throwing the covers from his lower half and swinging his legs over the side of the bed like he's going to leave before we can finish this conversation. His shoulders rise with a breath before he looks back at me and says, "Okay, then tell me what you want, Tate."

Why would he say that? Isn't it obvious? I want this. Him. It's what I wanted for a long time, but I spent so long telling myself it was impossible. And now, it's right in front of me. All I have to do is reach out and grab it. So, why can't I?

"Thought so," he says and pushes out of bed. "When you figure it out, then we'll have a conversation."

"It's you," I say, and it pauses his steps briefly. "I want *you*, Braxton."

"Don't say that." Braxton shakes his head, resuming his retreat to the bathroom. "The only reason you're even thinking about this is because of this stupid predicament we're in. Would you have ever given this a second thought had I not—"

"If not for this 'stupid predicament,' I would've never learned the truth!" I climb out of bed and meet him in the middle of the room, halfway to the bathroom. "You could've saved us both a role in the Farrah and Micah show had you just—"

"I already told you, Tate. It wasn't my place. I'm not a child. I wasn't going to walk up and say, 'You stole my toy,' because he got to you first."

"So you date my best friend instead?"

Braxton scoffs, scrubbing a hand down his face, and I

get the feeling I'm missing something. "She came to me. I didn't even look twice at Farrah until she asked me on a date because *she* thought it would be fun to do double dates and things together."

She…went to him? But she told me Braxton had practically begged her to go on a date with him.

"By that time, I had convinced myself I wasn't in love with you. I told myself…I only wanted what Micah had, and I thought I could have it with Farrah."

"You loved me?" A small ache forms in my chest, and it only intensifies when he doesn't say anything. "Answer the question, Braxton."

He sighs. "I don't know."

What does that mean? How can he possibly not know if he loved me back then? Does he still love me?

The loud vibrations of my phone buzzing on the nightstand catch our attention, and I do my best to ignore it, knowing who is on the other end. "Braxton—"

"You need to go," he says, pulling his sweater over his head and walking out the door.

Steam rising off my skin, I step over the shower threshold onto the white mat, careful to avoid the tile floor as I reach for my towel on the wall. Twisting my hair into the towel, I step forward onto the second mat in front of the sink and notice the small paths rushing down the length of the mirror, only providing a small sliver of my reflection. The woman who stares back at me looks…different. More relaxed than the one who arrived a few days ago. Partly from the spa day earlier, but it's not the only reason. There's a small—okay, maybe a little more than small—part of me knows it has to do with the man I woke up next to this morning. Even if he did walk out on me...again.

I roll my eyes at the thought and reach for the stack of clothes on the—*Shit.*

"You've got to be kidding me," I whisper to the empty air. How could I forget my clothes?

I groan and unravel my hair from the towel before wrapping it around my frame. Braxton wasn't here when I got back, and I wasn't in the shower too long...I should be safe, but still, I need to make this quick.

Less than sixty seconds to get from the bathroom door to the closet, open the door, and finger through the hangers until I find my dress...but it's not enough time for me to get to the bathroom before I hear the beep from the other side and the whirl of the locking mechanism. The door swings open. Braxton pauses in the doorway before quickly stepping inside and closing the door. His jaw locks, and he fights to keep his gaze from traveling down my barely clothed body.

"We've got to stop meeting like this," he says with a slight chuckle, taking a few steps forward.

I don't answer, instead draping my dress over my shoulder and walking back to the bathroom. Still annoyed with the reminder that he walked out earlier after accusing me of not knowing what I want, I take my time getting ready, starting with my hair and then my makeup before finally pulling on my dress.

This time, when I walk out of the bathroom, he doesn't stop his eyes from tracing over every inch of my figure. I watch his tongue poke out slightly before he rolls his lips between his teeth as he comes to the high slit, showing off my left thigh. The look in his eyes fans the flames deep within my core, but I do my best to ignore them. He's the one who walked out. Twice! I'm not going to throw myself at someone who doesn't want—

"Looking for this?" Braxton asks, breaking my thoughts. He stands, fingering the gold lipstick tube I'd just been looking for. I reach for it, trying to snatch it from his hands, but he doesn't let go. What is it with him and not letting go of my things? "Tay," he says at the same time I use his name as my own plea for him to release his grasp.

"We don't have time for this," I say, choosing to ignore the pleading look in his eyes.

When I think he's going to let go, he doesn't. Braxton takes a step closer and plants a hand firmly on my hip. "Tell me why you're mad."

"I'm not mad."

"Okay," he drawls. "Tell me why you're upset, then."

"I'm not upset."

"Yes, you are, and I'm just trying to understand."

I glare up at him. He's trying to *understand*? I don't have the time necessary for this conversation right now. I'm supposed to be downstairs for the rehearsal. But you know what? Maybe the third time is the charm.

"Where do I even start?" I scoff and take two steps back. "There is so much going on right now, so many thoughts swirling in my head, and every one of them revolves around *you*. First, it was how we had to tell Farrah about Micah. And then, you show up here and pull me into this sick game of pretending to be together. Then I find out you've been lying to me for years. And that you loved me but never told me." I take a deep breath and fight back the stinging sensation forming in the corners of my eyes. I don't have time to redo my makeup. I cannot let my emotions get the best of me. "How could you not tell me all of this, Braxton? Why didn't Jason tell me before he died? Why did you let me stay with Micah? You could've saved us all a lot of bullshit the last few years if you'd just said something."

It's Braxton's turn to scoff. He shakes his head as his tongue wets his lips again. "Oh, Pretty Girl, you have no idea how hard it was. How many times I had to stop myself from saying something, doing something...To watch you give yourself to him, over and over again, and to watch him break you. You gave him everything, Tate, and he gave you nothing. But God forbid I say something about it. Confront him for the way he treated you...Because when I did, I was just jealous. I was *bitter* because he got the girl, and I didn't. I thought—I thought if I said something to you, you would think the same." Soft eyes meet mine, and I feel the same ache in my chest from this morning return tenfold. "So many times I thought about it—thought about telling you despite the fear—but what good would it have done? For either of us. I wasn't about to become who he said I was. And you were in love with him, you—"

"What if I wasn't?"

And I wasn't. I know that now.

"Yes, you were, Tate," Braxton says. "We all saw it. And it killed me to have a front row seat to it. To watch you love him and force yourself into the box he and his parents created for you. The best thing you ever did was join EWE. If it wasn't for that company, I don't know if you ever would've gotten out."

"I wasn't, Braxton. That wasn't love. I only stayed with him because of *Jason*. Because I knew he wouldn't introduce me to someone unless he thought it was a good fit...If you had just said something—"

"What was I supposed to say, huh?" He takes a step closer. "Was I supposed to walk up and tell you that you were supposed to meet me that night? Act like a toddler whose toy got stolen? What would you have thought of me then?"

That's not him. That's not who he is, even if right now I'm wishing it was.

"That's not me, Tay," Braxton says. "That's not you, either. And to some degree, I thought maybe Micah was right. I was only searching—yearning—for what he had. Thought I was just jealous because he got to you first…I told myself it wasn't you I wanted. I just wanted what you guys had. You were only a placeholder for my idea of love and commitment."

"So, you don't have feelings for me?" I ask, but he doesn't answer, and the silence is maddening. "Stop it. Stop doing that! Answer me, Braxton."

He sighs. "I thought I was over it. I thought…I thought it was done. But then, I saw you in the coffee shop and…"

"If you felt this way, why did you get engaged to Farrah?"

"I was happy enough with her, I convinced myself that was the next step," he says with a small shrug. "I thought we were happy. I thought she was happy. I'd given her everything she wanted. Hell, I'd even given up my friends for her. I did everything she asked to become the person she wanted me to be…but it still wasn't enough for her. She wanted him. She always wanted him, but he had you."

"And where did I fall in all of this? What about me? What about what I wanted?"

"You didn't want—"

"Stop telling me what I want!" I can't contain my outburst, and he freezes. "I wanted you, Braxton. It should've been you, but I wasn't given the option. That choice was made for me before I ever walked into that bar."

His gaze narrows.

"You weren't just one of Micah's best friends, you were mine, too. And I fell in love with you." I drop my face into my hands, shaking my head slightly. I can't believe I'm going to say this…to admit this. I've never said this to anyone. Not my sister, not my mom, not Savvy or any of the other girls. This was the one thing I swore I'd take to the grave. "I told myself it was wrong, and I told myself it was only because Micah was an asshole sometimes. But the truth is, that wasn't true at all. I was just scared to do something about it because I thought

I'd be letting Jason down. I thought you didn't want me. You had other girlfriends and dates, and hookups, and then there was Farrah." I told myself it was just because he was nice to me, and I had been spending too much time with him and around him. So, I did what any good girlfriend would do, and I put some distance between the two of us. "I had no choice but to push everything aside, especially when you chose her."

"You chose first, Tate."

"Because I didn't know better! I wanted you, Bray."

Braxton shakes his head. "Don't say that."

"Why? Why are you so afraid to hear the truth?" I ask, but he only stands there, hands shoved deep into the pockets of his gray slacks. He doesn't say anything, doesn't look like he's going to say anything, and truthfully, the lack of response hurts.

I sigh, wiping my palms on the sides of my dress. This is going nowhere. We're just going in circles, always coming back to this same sentiment, and I don't have time for it right now. I was supposed to be downstairs two minutes ago.

"I don't have time for this. I have to go," I say, stuffing my lipstick into my purse and securing the strap on my shoulder.

"Tate, don't—" He finally calls out, but I'm already out the door.

12

Braxton

Her laughter fills the space from across the room, but the smile doesn't quite reach her eyes. The black satin halter-top dress she wears is sophisticated and sexy. The long slit up her left thigh that leads into the asymmetrical hemline makes it hard to control the thoughts racing through my mind. From the moment she stepped out of the bathroom earlier, all I wanted to do was rip the damn thing off her and lock the door. Instead, I'm forced to watch as she keeps her distance because she's still upset with me...and rightfully so, I suppose. I hate that we had that argument before this. I hate that I added more stress to her plate when the past few days have been nothing short of a circus.

Take tonight, for example. I arrived not long after the start of the rehearsal, taking a seat in the back row to stay out of the way, but still with a view of her. I watched as Farrah tried not to freak out because they had to start the rehearsal *without* the groom. Where was Micah? No one seemed to know. The wedding planner's assistant became the stand-in groom, while the bridesmaids fought over their order, and the mothers of the bride and groom chastised the planner for not having things in order. The entire time, Tate stood off to the side with her arms crossed, face pulled into a tight line, waiting for someone to take control of the situation.

Now, for a brief moment, her eyes catch mine. I offer her a small smile, and she does the same before returning to her conversation with one of Farrah's aunts—the nice one. That's how it's been all night, small gestures to show those around us that nothing is wrong, but on the inside, I know there's a storm brewing.

This display we've had to put on has worn me out. I was never supposed to be here—never wanted to be—and I never meant to put Tate in this position or expose the truth from all those years ago. Still, hearing her admission earlier shocked me. At the risk of being a cliché, it knocked the breath from my lungs. I never imagined she'd feel the same, or that she could have felt the same at one point. Damn me and my morals. If only I could be more like Micah, maybe we could've avoided all of this bullshit the last few years...But before I could think of what to say next, she was gone, racing out the door back to the people who always seemed to be in the way of us getting what we both wanted.

"You have a minute?" a quiet, restrained voice asks from beside me at the bar. *Micah.*

I scoff. "No, not really."

"We need to talk."

"I'm not sure what there is to talk about, Mick," I say, taking the glass of whiskey from the bartender. "I'm not here for you, okay? I'm just here to support that woman over there." A glance over my shoulder shows Tate leaning into a one-armed hug from the aunt. This time, a real smile spreads across her red lips.

"Oh, right, you're here for *her*. Who you conveniently forgot to mention you were dating when we talked a few weeks ago."

"Why would I tell you that?" I ask, taking a sip of my drink.

"Why would you—Because she's my ex-girlfriend!" Micah can barely contain his outburst, catching the attention of a few partygoers walking by. He glares at them, and they quickly avert their stares and pick up their pace.

"Exactly," I say. "Your *ex*-girlfriend. As in the past. As in you're not dating her now. You haven't been with her in over three years. Why does it matter if she and I date?"

He glares up at me, and I notice the slight tint of red in the corners of the whites of his eyes. Taking another sip, I set a ten-dollar bill down on the bar and walk away. Micah follows hot on my heels and forces me into one of the private dining rooms, away from the rest of the party.

"Why are you here?" Micah practically spits out between gritted teeth once the door closes. "And don't feed me the same shit you've been feeding everyone else. What are you really doing here?"

"I don't know what you want me to say, man. I'm here for Tate. That's it."

And that's God's honest truth. If it wasn't for her, I wouldn't be standing here.

"Bullshit." He scoffs. "Did you think you could come here and convince Farrah not to go through with the wedding? Are you and Tate in on this together? Some scheme to ruin my marriage before it even gets started?"

"I don't think you need any help with that," I say, doing my best not to laugh. "But you'd probably like that, so you have someone else to blame other than yourself."

His eyes narrow. "What's that supposed to mean?"

"What do you think is going to happen when Farrah finds out you've been gambling all your money, and probably hers, away again, Mick? Because that's what you've been doing, isn't it? That's why you came and asked me—"

"Shut up!" Micah jabs his finger in my direction. "Shut the fuck up."

"Oh, that hit a nerve, didn't it?"

"This is ridiculous! You don't know anything. You don't know anything, but somehow you always seem to think you do. Did you drag Tate into this because—"

"Oh, don't try and act like you care about her."

"I do care about her."

"That's why you dumped her? For choosing to follow her dreams?"

"She didn't need to do that bullshit. Do you know how embarrassing it was to tell people my girlfriend was a professional wrestler? I used to get so much shit from the guys at the office and my parents. They couldn't stand that she was—"

"That sounds like a you problem."

"I didn't see you stepping up to the plate," he says, and it deflates the swell in my chest a little. "Oh, that's right, because you were still fucking her best friend. The closest thing you would ever get to the real thing. That's why you dated Farrah in the first place. Isn't it? Because you couldn't have Tate, so you went to the next best thing."

"Farrah pursued me, not the other way around. That had nothing to do with Tate," I say.

"You know something..." Micah taps his finger against his chin, pacing a few steps in front of me. "I find it funny that you guys suddenly started dating right before my wedding. Not to mention, Tate never said anything to Farrah. That doesn't seem like her. Usually, she tells Farrah everything."

"You know what I think is funny? You're doing all of this to cover your ass. You have a problem, Micah. A real problem, and you refuse to admit it. You refuse to get help." Too many times in the past, I had this same conversation with him, but just like now, he rolls his eyes and pretends like I'm being irrational. "Why come to me? If you really needed the money for the wedding, why not go to your parents? Or her parents? Why come to me? Or Tate?"

"I never went to Tate." He seems taken aback by the accusation.

"No," I say, shaking my head. "Farrah did."

His eyes widen, and he still seems genuinely surprised. "What?"

"Farrah came to Tate for a loan because she said you guys were short. Then, a few months later, you come to me for the same damn thing. Seems a little suspicious, doesn't it?"

"I didn't—I didn't know that." Micah shakes his head, scrubbing a hand down his face. He sighs. "She said—Why would she go to Tate?"

"Probably for the same reason you came to me," I say, and watch as he tries to steady his breathing, tugging on the ends of his hair. "You're fucking pathetic. Grow up, Micah. You're over thirty years old; it's time to be a man."

"A man?" A dark chuckle follows. "Is that what you think you are? Braxton, I hate to break it to you, but you're a pathetic excuse for one. I've seen the way she is with you, and trust me, it won't be long."

What the fuck does that mean?

"Take tonight, for example," he continues. "She's barely even looked at you. Barely spoken to you. Forty-eight hours around me, and she's already forgotten you again."

My jaw clenches, and my grip tightens around the glass in my hands.

His chuckle only makes my jaw clench harder. I can hear my teeth scrape beneath the pressure.

"Isn't it funny how you're still the second choice? Jason never fucking wanted you around. You were a thorn in our side. Tate never wanted you. She *chose* me when she was supposed to choose you. And Farrah, well, Farrah chose me long before you chose her."

Did he just admit to sleeping with Farrah while we were together?

"If you wanted Farrah so bad, why didn't you just end things with Tate?" I ask.

"Because I knew you wanted her."

My heart stops, and the answer hangs between us. The truth is finally out. He never wanted Tate. He only wanted to make sure I couldn't have her. Because he couldn't stand the fact that Jason would think someone other than Micah deserved the pretty girl. And the moment Jason and I walked into the bar that night, Jason immediately regretted saying anything to Micah in the first place.

"You weren't even supposed to be there. You were supposed to be at your parents' anniversary dinner," I say.

"I showed my face, shook hands with a few people, and dipped," Micah says, shoulders rising in a nonchalant shrug. "She didn't want you, Braxton. She never wanted you."

That's not true. I know it's not true. She just told me—

"She needed someone who could show her the way of the world. Someone who could bring her head out of the clouds and her ass out of that damn ring."

"And how did that turn out?"

Micah glowers at me, and all I see before me is the same spoiled brat I've known almost all my life. "You will always be second best, Braxton. You can *play* the hero all you want, but deep down, you'll always know I was her first choice. She loved me first. And if I offered her the chance, you know she'd pick me again. You're just what she's settling for because—"

"If I were you, I'd watch what you say next," a voice dripping thick with venom sounds behind me. I glance over my shoulder to find Tate inside the doorway. How long has she been standing there? Her eyes blaze with fury, but beneath all of that anger is a sadness I've only seen once, when Jason died. His unexpected death hit us all hard, but for Tate, it hit harder. Jason and Judah were like the brothers she never had growing up. Losing him devastated her. That same hurt hides beneath the fury as she closes the distance between her and Micah. "You are the same fucking prick you've always been, Micah. And you know something? The two of you were fucking made for each other."

What is going on? The two of who?

"You were a mistake, Micah. Every day that I spent with you was one wasted. You weren't a fucking choice, you were a roadblock. And had I been given the option seven years ago, I sure as hell wouldn't have chosen you. But him?" For the first time since she walked into the private dining room, she looks at me, and a soft smile graces her lips. "I'd choose him every day."

I hold her stare as her words crash down on me. *I'd choose him every day.*

"Tate, baby, c'mon. You don't—" Micah reaches out toward her, but she rips her arm away from his grasp.

"Does she know?"

He scoffs. "I don't know what you're talking about."

"Does Farrah know you're gambling again? Did she come to me and ask for money *knowing* the truth about why you were short on cash?"

Micah straightens his shoulders and lifts his chin. "I didn't even know she came to you."

"Oh, feed your bullshit to someone else, Micah."

"She didn't tell me! She told me she got it from her mom. I would never let her come to you about something like that."

Tate glances my way, but I can only shrug. Micah seemed genuinely shocked when I told him.

"Does she know you're gambling again?" she asks a second time.

"Again?" Micah scoffs, a smirk spreading across his face.

"Sweetie, I never stopped." His condescending tone irks me, along with the use of the pet name, and when he takes a step closer to Tate, I do the same.

"Does she know?" Tate asks again.

"She doesn't *need* to know."

"You're unbelievable. Micah, you can't do this. You have to tell her."

"I don't have to tell her shit."

"She's about to be your wife!"

"Exactly! And at least Farrah knows her place, unlike you."

That cuts her deep. I can see it in the way her face falls and she loses a bit of the fire inside her. Stepping between them, I wrap my arm around Tate, putting her behind me. "Don't you dare speak to her that way," I say.

Micah takes another step forward, finger pointing into my face. "Stay out of this, Braxton. You aren't—"

"Get your hand out of my face before I break it."

"I'll have you arrested for assault."

"Good, I'll be sure to tip Sheriff Rhodes off to your other, more miscellaneous activities." My brow cocks, and his eyes widen. Micah's drug problem isn't as well known in his circle of friends, or maybe everyone still looks the other way, kind of like they do with the gambling. "Did you think no one knew, Mick? You're a terrible liar and have the worst poker face of anyone I've ever played across from. That's what got you into this situation in the first place."

"Well, it's good enough to convince her I wasn't fucking her best friend for most of our relationship." Micah's eyes widen as the admission rolls off his tongue.

I wait for the explosion to come from behind me, but it never does. Instead, it's a quiet simmer, and when I turn to look at her, Tate's eyes are locked on the other man. She chuckles softly, humorlessly, before her mouth quirks up.

"Thank you," she says softly.

"Thank you?"

"For saving me from Farrah's bullshit excuses. Because no doubt, she'll try to tell me I 'misunderstood' or 'misheard' Bethany and the other girls saying how pathetic I am for being here. How unbelievable it is that I'm standing up beside Farrah when she's marrying my ex-boyfriend, the man she's been fucking behind my back for years."

"Tate—"

"Save your breath, Micah." Her voice is heavy, exhausted. "I'm done with you, both of you. I refuse to stand up there and—"

"No! Tate, please. You have to."

"I don't have to do shit. Why would I stand up there knowing the truth?"

"Because if you don't, Farrah will lose her shit. And I can't...I can't handle a Frost meltdown right now. You're her best friend. You're the maid of honor!"

"You're unbelievable. Truly, Micah, unbelievable. You want me to pretend like nothing is wrong? Like, I didn't just overhear her real besties gossiping about me? Like, you didn't just admit to cheating on me with my supposed best friend? You want me to smile and stand beside her while she marries you to save you from a fucking meltdown?" Tate scoffs, shaking her head. "No, fuck you. You deserve what's coming to you, Micah. You both do."

"Braxton, man, c'mon." He looks at me, a pleading look in his eyes, but when I refuse, he turns back to her. "Don't say anything, not yet. J-just give me until tomorrow. After the wedding. And the four of us can sit down and—"

"There you guys are!" And that's what I like to call Farrah timing. She always seems to show up right on time. I watch Micah's eyes grow to the size of dinner plates before the woman of the hour completes our circle. She looks around at the three of us, and her smile slips slightly. "What's going on?"

Tate and Micah continue to glare at one another. I'm the only one who acknowledges her presence, meeting her questioning gaze.

"Braxton?" Farrah asks, but I ignore her.

"Tate," I say, slipping my hand in Tate's. "C'mon, let's go."

"Go?" Farrah practically chokes on the word. "Where are you going? Someone tell me what in the hell is going on."

"Do you want to tell her or should I?" Tate asks Micah, still glaring at him.

"Would somebody tell me what in the hell is happening?" Farrah begs.

"Fine, I will," Tate says, turning toward the other woman.

"Tay," I stop her, squeezing her hand. She looks up at me, and I motion toward the door where a small crowd has started to form—at the front, the other bridesmaids and mothers of the bride and groom. Using our intertwined hands, I pull her into my chest and kiss her temple. "Not here. Not right now."

Tate sighs in defeat. This is not the time or place to have this conversation, whether they deserve it or not. That's not who we are, not to mention someone in that crowd is sure to pull out their phone and record the chaos destined to unfold the moment Tate confronts Farrah. There are a million reactions she could have, and most of them aren't appropriate for someone of Tate's status.

"What is going on?" Farrah asks, leaning into Micah.

"N-nothing," he wavers before clearing his throat. "Everything is fine, Fay."

"Don't fucking lie to me, Mick. I know—"

"We need to talk," Tate interrupts. "Tomorrow morning."

"Tomorrow morning?" Farrah scoffs, turning around. "Tate, we're supposed to—"

"Honestly, Farrah, I don't give a fuck."

Farrah's face falls into a thin line, the mask of a concerned fiancé and friend disappearing almost immediately, and I can't help but wonder if she knows exactly what this is about. She straightens her shoulders and crosses her arms over her chest. "Fine."

"Fine," Tate answers.

Neither one backs down, though. Neither wants to be the first to walk away. Stubborn asses, I think, and catch the look Micah gives me. He's thinking the same thing. He unwinds Farrah's arms from her chest and whispers something in her ear. For a brief moment longer, she glares at Tate before she finally relinquishes, the mask put back in place right before our eyes. She gives a simple nod to her mother, and Mrs. Frost immediately takes over the situation.

"Okay, everyone, this is just a little misunderstanding," Maggie says, ushering everyone out of the doorway. "Friends sharing a private conversation of congratulations. Let's give them a moment, huh?"

Farrah shares a final glance with Tate before stalking off, Micah trailing behind her with his eyes glued to the floor.

When the door closes behind them, it's quiet for a moment, and Tate pulls her hand from mine, taking a deep breath. She winds her arms around her torso, and I start to reach for her, but she's already gone.

The moment she steps outside onto the snow-covered patio, Tate takes a deep breath of fresh mountain air. I'm two steps behind her, catching the door right before it slams, and when I walk outside, the sight breaks my heart. Tate folds in on herself, face buried in her hands as she tries to contain herself a little while longer. I don't know if she wants me here, but I take a step closer anyway, draping my jacket over her bare shoulders and pulling her into my arms. Relief floods through me when she doesn't fight me; instead, she leans into my embrace.

"I'm so sorry, Pretty Girl," I whisper against her temple. A quiet sob escapes her. "You deserve better than this, Tay. Better than them. You always have."

Her shoulders shake slightly as she finally lets go of the pent-up frustration and anger she's been holding back. The hurt that comes from knowing your supposed best friend has been lying to you for years. I'm not sure how long we stand there, maybe three or four minutes, long enough that I feel the chill seep into the fabric of my button-up. Tate pulls away, wiping beneath her eyes, trying not to smear her makeup any more than it already is.

"Did you know?"

"About them messing around?" I confirm, and she nods. "I had my suspicions, but never anything concrete enough to call them out...Not until Micah admitted it tonight."

Even though most of her face is covered by my shadow, I can see her eyes narrow. I have to be careful. She's still in a volatile space, and I don't want to set her off.

"Why didn't you tell me?" Tate asks.

"I didn't *know*," I say, putting more emphasis on the last word. "I couldn't prove anything. I only had suspicions because of how they acted around each other. People used to say the same thing about us, too, Tate. They said the same things, and I knew we weren't doing anything...I couldn't afford to be wrong. It wasn't until she jumped ship for him immediately after he came back to Snowhaven that I felt like everything was confirmed..."

"So, why didn't you—"

"You guys had been broken up for over a year. I wasn't about to drag you back into this."

Her mouth twitches slightly, and I see the tears well in her eyes again, but she rips her gaze from mine. "I hate them," she whispers.

I gently reach up to turn her face back to me, tucking a strand of hair behind her ear. The tears line her eyes, threatening to spill over, and my thumb swipes away one that breaks free. "No, you don't. You love them, and that's why it hurts so much."

"Why aren't you more upset?"

"Because I've had my time to be upset. I already grieved what I lost here a long time ago. But for you..." I wipe another tear that falls. "This is like ripping off the Band-Aid on a wound that never fully healed. That's okay. You're allowed to feel it, to go through the motions, to grieve. You need to, or you'll never be able to move on."

Tate buries her face into my chest, and I wrap my arms around her, resting my chin on the top of her head.

"If that means you need to cry, then cry. You want to yell at someone? Yell at me. You want to scream? There's a mountain right there willing to take it. The only thing I ask is that you don't hold it all inside."

"I'm sorry for being a brat earlier," she mumbles.

I laugh and pull back slightly, cradling her face between my hands. "You weren't a brat. You're just trying to put the pieces together. So am I. We're in this together, Tay."

"But what happens when we leave?"

"Well..." I sigh. "I guess that depends on what you want."

"What about what you want?"

"Whatever you decide, Taylor...that's what I want," I say, letting my thumb trace along her bottom lip. Because as much as it would hurt to let her walk away again, I'd let her go if that's what she wanted.

"You know what I really want?" Tate asks, rolling her bottom lip between her teeth. "Pizza."

13

Tate

Crisp bubbles coat my taste buds when I take a sip of the liquid gold inside my glass, trying to hide my giggles from Braxton. He's recounting a story from one of the job sites his team has worked on. The last time I saw him, he was simply a foreman, but now he owns the company. This particular story involves a property with an owner who had an abnormal amount of screws all over his house.

"I swear," Braxton continues. "When my foreman asked him about it, he said, 'Gotta keep all my loose screws in one place.'"

This time, I laugh out loud, not bothering to contain myself.

We're still dressed in our rehearsal dinner attire. I couldn't be bothered to change after we returned from our run into town for a pizza from Nick's Pizza Parlor. Instead, I sat on the floor, stretching my legs out before me, and popped the bottle of champagne I ordered at the front desk on our way out the door. Braxton told me the mixture of champagne and pizza was disgusting, but I told him to trust me. It's surprisingly good and has become one of my comfort meals over the years. Not that it's the best choice, but it tastes good and that's all that matters.

"He did not," I say, still giggling.

"I thought they were fucking with me. I didn't see anything like that when I was there, but when I went with them the next day...lo and behold, there they were. *Everywhere.*"

"Was he fucking with you guys?"

Braxton shrugs. "Who knows. Maybe? Seems like a lot of trouble just to fuck with the guys fixin' up your kitchen, though."

A final laugh bubbles in my chest before I sigh, and I lean my head back against the foot of the bed. I swirl the champagne around the glass, bringing it to my lips and downing what's left. It was my first and only glass of the evening. I had decided against drinking at the rehearsal dinner because... well, truthfully, because I wasn't in the mood. That probably sounds abnormal, but the last thing I wanted was alcohol in my system if Braxton decided to finish our conversation from earlier. Little did I know he wasn't the one I'd have to worry about.

"You okay, Pretty Girl?" His voice pushes through my clouded thoughts.

"No, but I will be," I say, eyes glued to the ceiling. The heat of his stare bores into the side of my face, and finally, I let my gaze fall to meet his again. "Why do you call me that?"

His brow arches in question.

"Pretty Girl...What made you start calling me that? You've never called me that before."

Braxton only stares for a moment before a smile lifts the corner of his mouth, and he chuckles. "I, uh, I don't know. I guess it's because I always thought you were pretty. Not the made-up kind of pretty, but the raw and real kind. From the second I saw you in that bar years ago, you just lit up the space, and I've always thought you were the prettiest girl in any room."

I roll my eyes but can't fight my own smile. "You're a suck-up."

"I can call you something else if you prefer," he says. "*Honeybun*, perhaps? *Snookums*?"

My laughter from earlier returns full force as he continues to list off pet names. He leans over, poking my side gently, and it only makes me laugh harder when he hits a sensitive spot.

"*Pookie*? Oh, that's a good one." Another poke, this time lightly digging into the spot in a soft tickle. "*Baby cakes*? Oh, yeah, that's the one."

I squeal when his fingers wrap around my sides, tickling me full force. "Bray, stop!"

The air stills, and so do his hands, before our eyes meet, and I realize just how close we are. All it would take is for one of us to lean forward, filling the small space between us. My breaths come out in hard pants, like I'm trying to catch my breath. Clearing my throat, I pull away slightly, but not far enough. I can still feel the heat radiating off his body, his hands still gripping my waist. "I, uh…You know, I wanted to thank you. I know this wasn't easy for you, but—"

"Pfft." Braxton blows a raspberry. "What do you mean? I've had the time of my life. Who wouldn't want to hang out with their ex-best friend, ex-fiancée, and their families to celebrate their impending nuptials? It's everything I ever wanted for Christmas." He chuckles to himself, and I roll my eyes. "You know something?" This time, when I meet his gaze, all evidence of his joking seconds ago is gone. Braxton leans in again, and he's so close I smell the mixture of mint, tomato paste, and whiskey on his breath. "This has been the weirdest

Christmas of my life, but I'd do it all over again for you."

His lips gently brush against mine, and when I don't pull away, he closes the gap. A fire ignites in my veins, and I feel my heartbeat strengthen in my chest. He slowly cradles my face in one hand, the other winding around my torso to pull me even closer as he nips at my bottom lip and I open to him. His tongue sweeps over mine in long, languid strokes, and he takes his time, as if committing every inch of me to memory. Slowly, Braxton lifts me off the floor onto his lap and groans when I involuntarily grind against him. The sound goes straight to my core.

Sitting upright, I reach around and undo the clasp at the back of my neck that holds the halter top together, letting the top of my dress fall. His hazel eyes grow dark, and his throat bobs as he stares at my bare chest. His tongue sneaks out past his lips, rolling back the flesh between his teeth before his gaze lifts to mine, asking permission, and I nod.

Braxton cups my right breast, kneading the flesh in hands roughened by years of manual labor. He tweaks my nipple between his thumb and forefinger before bending to capture it in his mouth, suckling on the already sensitive peak. I gasp, digging my fingers through his hair and pulling him even closer as his tongue swirls around me, followed by soft bites. I buck my hips against him, earning another groan in return. This time, though, I don't stop and begin to move my body in a slow, fluid motion against his. With each cycle, I feel him getting harder beneath me.

He releases my nipple with a subtle pop and rests his head back against the side of the bed, eyes screwed shut. "Are you trying to make me come in my pants, Pretty Girl?"

"Actually, I'd prefer if you come in me."

Braxton all but whines. "Fuck, Tay." His gaze lowers back to mine, pupils blown wide, making his eyes appear devoid of all color. There's a hunger in them that matches the aching need inside me. I've dreamed about this moment countless times. Dreamed of the day he'd show up on my doorstep and tell me the last seven years had been a mistake, that it should've been him that night. Rough hands skim my shoulders, tracing a line all the way down my arm and back up before reaching around behind me. His fingers toy with the back of my dress, gently tugging on the fabric to pull it out from under me. Every pull against my skin sends a shiver down my spine. "If you have any reservations, I need you to speak now or forever hold your peace, because I don't know how much longer I'll be able to control myself. I have to start making up for lost time."

His name rolls off my tongue when one of his hands moves to cup me through my underwear—the only thing between me and his greedy fingers. Slowly, they circle my entrance over the fabric, and I gasp at the feeling. It's so light, yet heavy at the same time, and shockingly intimate.

"Fuck, baby. You're so fucking wet for me. You've soaked through your underwear." Braxton moves his hand again, slipping his fingers past the band, and I gasp when he makes contact. He circles my clit, and I cling to him. His breath is hot and warm against my neck as his fingers continue their work. I roll my hips against his hand, desperately seeking more friction, but instead of giving me what I need, he removes his hand. Braxton brings his wet fingers to his mouth, and I can't take my eyes off him as he licks them clean. "Last chance, Pretty Girl. If you want me to stop—"

"No." I claw at his shoulders, earning a raspy chuckle in reply. "You've made me wait long enough, Braxton Powell. Don't you dare stop."

Goosebumps rise across my skin as his fingers trail down my arm and brush against the side of my breast. Braxton fingers my dress for a brief moment before, without warning, he winds his arms around my waist and stands up. I squeal, burying my face into the side of his neck, before he sets me on the edge of the bed. "Sit still, baby. I want another taste."

Braxton drops to his knees before me and lifts the back of my hand to his lips before he grips my thighs and pulls me even closer to the edge. The force sends me back onto the bed, and he tugs my dress and underwear down my legs. He bends down, pressing a lingering kiss to my inner thigh before I feel his teeth caress the skin. When he bites down, my body jolts, making him chuckle.

"Relax, Tate. You'd think you've been waiting seven years or something."

"Fuck off," I breathe out, but that breath morphs into a moan when his tongue trails up my thigh to my core. Braxton brushes his nose over my clit and breathes in. When he exhales, I gasp as he blows against my entrance. One finger swipes up my center, but it's the first swipe of his tongue that arches my back off the duvet. "Holy shit."

Braxton groans in response before his hands cement my thighs in place, and he runs his tongue up my center again. Slow strokes lap up my arousal and draw me closer to the edge. Every two or three licks, he flicks my clit. A quiet flame builds in my abdomen, and every time he flicks the sensitive bundle of nerves, it only adds fuel to that fire. I try to wiggle my hips, try to move against his mouth, but his hands hold me in place, forcing me to accept only what he gives, and the pace is agonizing.

I cry out when he pushes two fingers inside me, and I can feel his smile against my core. I lift my head to stare down at him, and normally I'd be embarrassed to meet the gaze of a man between my thighs, but not this time. Braxton's eyes lift to meet mine as he flattens his tongue and drags it slowly against my clit, his fingers curling inside me, and my breath comes out in hard pants. Still holding my gaze, he begins to quicken his pace, and a blush creeps up my neck into my cheeks. I tell myself to look away, but I can't, almost like I'm under a spell. His spell. And I never want it to end. When his tongue dips inside me, I cry out and grab his hair, yanking him closer. "Fuck, Braxton. Yes! Don't stop."

And he doesn't.

I brace myself on one forearm so I can continue to watch as he fucks me with his tongue. The sight is magical. When he replaces his tongue with two fingers again, he sucks my clit into his mouth and curls his fingers, hitting that sweet spot. And soon, I'm riding the waves of ecstasy as I come in his mouth.

Braxton's hands brace against my legs when I try to squeeze them shut. My body quakes beneath him as he laps up all of my orgasm with a hearty moan. He pulls away with a slight chuckle, and I hear the sound of clothing hitting the floor before I open my eyes to see him standing half naked at the end of the bed. His fingers make slow work of the buttons on his shirt, and his cock strains against the fabric of his underwear.

His shirt falls off his shoulders into the puddle of clothes at his feet before he shoves the cotton down his legs. *Fuck, he's big*, is the first thought that pops into my mind, and it's his girth that really stands out. He strokes the thick head of his cock before fisting the entire length with a low moan. My wide eyes must give away my thoughts when I look up to his face because Braxton smirks. "You'll be okay, Tay. I promise. Now, be a good girl and lie back against those pillows."

I do as I'm told without even thinking, dragging myself up the length of the bed until my back is pressed against the plump white pillows. Braxton crawls his way up the bed to meet me, pulling my legs so I come down a little, right where he wants me.

Braxton presses his lips against mine, and I taste myself. When he bites down on my lower lip, I open to him, our tongues caught in a dance of desperation and longing. His hand dips between my thighs, one finger slipping between my folds, and I moan. "You're still fucking soaked, baby." Pushing my thighs apart, he settles between them and lets the head of his cock brush against my entrance. "And you're going to take every bit of what I give you, right?"

I don't know if I can, but I nod my head.

"Watch, baby," he says, and looks between us as he pushes the tip of his cock in just a little, and I gasp at the feeling, because he feels even bigger than I thought. I don't get the chance to look before he pulls out. "Watch." His demand is met when I force my gaze down and watch as he strokes his length twice before pushing only the first inch inside me. "Fuck," Braxton breathes out, pushing in a little more and then pulling back out. He does it two more times before I look up under my lashes to watch him instead. Watch the way his eyes roll into the back of his head when he first pushes inside me, the way his tongue pokes out, wetting his lips before he pulls his bottom lip between his teeth and opens his eyes just in time to watch as he pulls out, rubbing the head against me.

"Bray, please." The words are strangled.

"What do you want, Pretty Girl?" The head of his cock rests at the edge of my aching core. "Say it."

"You." The word rolls off my tongue with ease. "I need all of you, Bray. Please." It's a desperate plea, and one that he's happy to oblige.

Braxton pushes inside me, this time with no hesitation or inhibition. The feeling is excruciating and heavenly all at the same time. He slowly eases in all the way, and I feel myself stretch to fit his girth completely until his hips meet mine, and he stills. He glances down at the space where our bodies are connected before I reach for him, pulling his mouth back to mine, and finally, he begins to move his hips. Braxton swallows every moan and curse I utter as his body rolls into mine like waves on a calm ocean, creating an agonizing rhythm.

I suck in a breath when he parts from me, trailing down my jaw and neck with his mouth. There's going to be a mark tomorrow, maybe two, but I don't care. Right now, I'd let him leave a hundred if it meant this never ended because it feels so damn good.

Braxton's hand reaches up to cup my breast, tweaking my nipple between his fingers. His other hand is splayed across my left thigh, hitching it up a little higher on his hips. My head falls back against the pillows, and a silent cry slips past my lips.

"God, you take me so good, Tate. I can't tell you how many times I touched myself at night just *thinking* of this moment. Thinking about when I'd finally be able to call you mine."

A soft whimper is my only reply.

He crashes his mouth down on mine again and sets a punishing pace. Each thrust is deeper and rougher than the last, snapping his hips forward as I beg him not to stop because it feels so fucking good. When he looks down at me, something clicks inside my chest. Something I can't quite name, but it feels like the final missing piece of my puzzle sliding into place. A quiet alignment that feels like coming home. He feels it, too, I'm sure of it.

I cling to him as I draw closer to the edge I've been chasing for a second time, legs wrapping around his waist and my hand trailing down between our bodies. My fingers move in circles around my swollen clit, reaching me higher and higher until I finally shatter. My body seizes beneath him, but I continue to move my fingers in a circular motion, chasing the rest of my high before I feel him tense.

"Tate," he groans.

"Come inside me, Bray," I say, and his eyes snap open.

His teeth are clenched so tight they could pressurize a fucking diamond. "I'm not wearing a condom."

"I. Don't. Care." I punctuate every word. I want to feel him come undone, to feel the warmth of his cum mixed with my own drip down my thighs. "I'll be fine, I have my own method of protection."

A breathy chuckle is his reply before his movements become sharp and erratic. Pulling almost all the way out and pushing back in, Braxton groans, his body going rigid as he fills me, fucking me through his own orgasm.

Braxton stays inside me, his forehead pressed against mine, as he softens before rolling to my side. He pulls me into his chest, hand resting on my hip, drawing invisible circles on my skin that send shivers down my spine. "I meant what I said," he whispers. "The past few days might just be the craziest thing I've ever done, and the weirdest, but I'd do it a thousand times if it meant getting to be with you."

My fingers ghost over his shoulder, coming in contact with the jagged little line that runs along the length of his collarbone. The skin is smoother than I imagined, but slightly pitted from where it was presumably stitched back together. It reminds me of the time we lost, and it reminds me that while we might be the same, we are completely different people from who we were seven years ago. "Where did you get this?"

He hums in acknowledgment. "What?"

"This scar. You never had it before."

Braxton gathers my hand into his, bringing it up to his mouth and kissing each fingertip lightly. "It was just a work accident."

"What happened?" I ask, propping myself up on my elbow.

He breathes out softly before opening his eyes to look up at me under weighted eyelids. "I fell off a ladder."

"You fell off a—"

"I'm fine, Tate." Braxton chuckles softly, more awake than he was seconds ago. "This was years ago, not long after Farrah and I broke up. I wasn't in a good headspace, and I wasn't paying attention. It's a little bit of a blur still, because I hit my head on the way down, but I ended up having to get a rod right here." He takes two of my fingers and presses them deeper into the skin, where I can feel a hard object along the bone.

"Does it hurt?"

He rolls his shoulder back, loosening the joint slightly. "Not usually, but it gets a little stiff from time to time, especially when it's cold."

"Well, as long as it wasn't something crazy like Micah stabbing you."

That makes his laugh boom around us. "I'd like to see him try."

14

Tate

WEDNESDAY, DECEMBER 25, 2019

A knock on the door draws my attention back to the bedroom. There's only one person it could be, but she isn't supposed to be here. I'm supposed to meet her in her room, but I should've known she would show up here instead. She can't risk someone overhearing our conversation. I step out of the bathroom, my toothbrush hanging out of my mouth, and Braxton looks at me over his shoulder as he walks toward the door. He offers me a small smile before I roll my eyes and return to the bathroom to finish brushing my teeth.

We spent a fair amount of time wrapped in the sheets last night and this morning before I forced myself out of bed to prepare for this exact moment, and I still don't feel ready. No matter what excuse Farrah plans to throw at me, I'm not going to the wedding. I refuse to stay somewhere I'm not wanted, and I won't stand beside someone on the most important day of their life if I'm not welcome there.

"I thought you wanted me to meet you upstairs," I say, walking out of the bathroom a minute later.

I'm shocked to see Farrah still dressed in her pajamas. She never goes anywhere unless she's dressed. She stands with her arms firmly crossed over her chest, hip popped to the side, a slight scowl on her face. "Honestly, I just want to get this over with."

Oh, how nice.

Braxton appears at my side, wrapping his arm around my waist, and kisses my forehead. "I'm gonna go. Let you two have some privacy."

"You don't have—"

"Yes, I do," he says, interrupting me. Braxton glances briefly at Farrah before turning back to me. "You two need to do this alone. I'll be back in just a few minutes, okay?"

There's a beat of silence when the door closes, following his departure. Farrah and I only stare at each other, and the weight of the last decade and a half washes over me. We met in high school, and I couldn't stand her. She was a touchy-feely kind of person, and I...wasn't. Slowly, though, we evolved into best friends, sisters, and when you thought of one of us, you always thought of the other. We've had our fair share of disagreements over the years, but in the last three years, I started to notice a rift between us. One that I've tried to bring up on more than one occasion, but Farrah always smiled and said things were fine. It wasn't convincing, but the more I pushed, the further she distanced herself. And finally, it came to the point where we've barely been speaking...unless she needs something. Still, I've stuck by her because that's what best friends do...right?

Farrah sighs. "So, are we just going to stand here, or are you going to tell me what this is about?"

"C'mon, Farrah." I scoff. "For once in your life, be honest."

"I don't—"

"Stop acting like everything between us is *fine*! It hasn't been fine for a long time, and I'm tired of you refusing to admit it. I have tried to talk to you, tried to understand what it is, but you always refuse to say what's on your mind. Now is the time, Fay."

Instead of a verbal response, her lips pull into a thin line, jaw set.

"Fine...You don't want to start? I'm going to ask you something, and I want you to be honest with me. Think you can do that?" Still, nothing. "Did you sleep with Micah?"

A flash of surprise crosses her features before her blue eyes flicker to the side.

"Were you sleeping with Micah while he and I were still together?"

Slowly, her gaze returns to mine, and she readjusts her stance but she still doesn't answer. She doesn't have to. I already know the answer. These questions are just confirmation of what I've already known.

I shake my head with a slight scoff. "You are such a bitch."

"He didn't want you, Tate." Farrah's words flood my entire body with heat, a fire burning so hot it's almost blinding. She hasn't said anything thus far, and that's what she's decided to start with?

"He didn't want...That doesn't make it okay, Farrah! That doesn't make any of this okay."

Farrah shrugs. "He was lonely. You weren't there. He needed someone who could be there for him. And clearly, that wasn't going to be you."

"I know I'm going to regret this," I say, pinching the bridge of my nose. "But how long was this going on?"

"Tate—"

"How long?" I snap.

Farrah stares at me, lips pursed, and gnaws on the inside of her cheek like she's going back and forth on whether or not to answer the question. After what feels like hours, she sighs and pushes a hand through her blonde waves. "Christmas of 2012."

"So, the whole fucking time. You've got to be kidding me, Farrah!" There's a small glimpse of what looks like remorse on her face, but it's gone just as fast. "Why didn't you just say something? He and I were together for almost four years after that. You started dating Braxton the next year. Why would you do that?"

"Because you wanted him." Her voice is small when she says it, so small that I can barely hear her. I'm not even sure I heard her correctly until she repeats herself, louder this time. "You wanted him, Tate. It was so obvious that you had feelings for Braxton. And you can't have both."

"But you can?"

Farrah rolls her eyes, pursing her lips. "I knew this was going to happen. I knew you were going to get all weird and jealous the closer we got to the wedding. Everyone told me not to invite you because it would make things awkward, but I didn't listen. And now, all week, I've realized they were right. I should've never invited you because you've—"

"You've got to be joking," I say, unable to stop myself.

"That's why I invited Braxton to stay! I thought it would make things easier for you, but if I'm being honest, it only made things worse. Not to mention how awkward it's been to sit across the dinner table from him. Did you ever stop to consider how that would make me feel?"

"How it would make—" I scoff. "Do you even hear yourself right now?"

"Faking the whole bag thing to get him up here, and then accidentally running into us in the lobby was a lot of work, when you could've just asked me if he could come," Farrah says. "To be quite honest with you, I didn't actually believe you were dating at first. I thought you had concocted this elaborate scheme to try to make Micah jealous so he'd call off the wedding."

It all makes sense now. That's why she put the mistletoe up last night. She wanted to see if we'd cave.

She scoffs, rolling her eyes. "But there's no way either of you is that good of an actor. Especially you. I've seen your Monday night segments."

I rub the space between my brow and sigh. This was a fucking mistake. She's not going to listen to a damn thing I say, and she refuses to be reasoned with.

With a heavy sigh, I repeat my words from earlier. "You're such a bitch."

But they still don't faze her. And why would they?

"For years, I've stuck up for you, made excuses for you when people say shit about you and Micah, but...I'm done," I continue. "I should've told you to fuck off the second you told me about Micah."

"Call me whatever you want, but you see who he's meeting at the end of the aisle today."

"This isn't a competition, Farrah!"

"You're just mad because I won."

Has she always been this delusional? What is it going to take to get this through her thick head?

"Yeah, and your prize is a fucking loser," I say. "He's broke, Farrah. Do you know what that means? That means no money, no savings, nothing. That means no more big country clubs, no more fancy dinners, no more—"

"You don't know what you're talking about," she says, too calmly for someone who has lived their entire life being waited on hand and foot. She grew up in a country club community. There's no way she'd be okay with this, unless...

"You know, don't you?" I ask, but she only stares at me. "About his gambling. And the drugs. You know."

Farrah straightens her shoulders and lets her face fall into a perfect line again.

"And you lied to me about it," I say, pointing my finger in her direction. "When I asked why you were short for the wedding…you said it was because of a client. You didn't speak to me for months, and then you not only had the audacity to call and ask me for a loan, but to lie about it."

"Well, I don't remember you telling me the truth about it in the past."

"Because it wasn't your business! You weren't his girlfriend, and I wasn't asking you for a loan."

"You could've warned me," she hisses, and I can see the string ready to snap inside of her. "I didn't even find out until he started pissing away all of the money my parents gave us for the wedding! You should've warned me, Tate, so I knew what I was getting into."

I laugh. "Do you hear yourself? You sound fucking delusional. You're lucky I didn't tell you to go fuck yourself when you called to tell me you were fucking my ex-boyfriend. The last thing on my mind was telling you about a problem I thought had been taken care of. But it's becoming clearer that his 'sabbatical' was just that—a nice, long vacation away from all of his responsibilities while his family cleaned up his mess. Again."

"Do you know he didn't even tell me he was leaving?"

Am I supposed to feel bad for her?

"He just disappeared for a year and then showed up one day out of the blue. Didn't even tell me he was back."

"That's why you said yes to Braxton," I say as the pieces begin to fall into place. She hadn't wanted Braxton, but now it makes sense why she said yes when he proposed. "Why would you want to get back together with someone who basically abandoned you for over a year? You had a perfectly good man who loved you, who would've—"

Farrah's laugh catches me off guard. "He didn't love me,

Tate. I was just a stand-in for you. It was so obvious that you and Braxton had a thing for each other, and if you did fuck around years ago, I can't say that I'd judge you. He is a good lay."

My fists ball up at my sides, and I cross my arms. I will not let her get the best of me. That's all she's trying to do by making that statement. It's just one more dig she's trying to get in before she leaves. "Braxton and I never hooked up, but I'm starting to understand why you were so worried about us," I say, and her brow cocks. "You were just projecting because you knew what you and Micah were doing was wrong."

"Oh, right, I forgot who I'm talking to. Miss Perfect. Miss Never-Does-Anything-Wrong." Farrah rolls her eyes. "Look, I don't know why you're so upset about all of this. Everyone got what they wanted. I got Micah, and you finally have Braxton. So, the road was a little bumpy to get here. Why does it matter?"

"Because it's the principle of it, Farrah!"

Farrah rolls her eyes again, falling onto the edge of the bed with her arms crossed tightly over her chest. "You're being ridiculous, Tate. Today is not supposed to be about you. It's supposed to be about *me*, but as always, you've decided that isn't going to fly."

I sigh. "You've got to be kidding me. God, everyone was right about you two."

"What are you talking about?"

"Everyone has always tried to tell me what terrible people you and Micah are, but I said they just didn't know you. They didn't know the Farrah that I know. They hadn't seen you on your worst days, hadn't seen you break down...Now I can't help but wonder what was real and what was some game of manipulation to get whatever you wanted out of me. You and Micah were made for each other."

"Well, at least you can admit it." She lifts her chin slightly and stands from her place on the bed. "Everyone got what they wanted, Tate. Why can't you just let this go and move on?"

"Did you?" I ask, and her gaze narrows. "Did you get *everything* you wanted, Farrah? Because if you ask me, you haven't looked happy once the entire time we've been here. If all you wanted was a big wedding, you could've married anyone!"

Farrah scoffs. "I'm happy with my choices. Not to mention, after this is all said and done, money won't be an issue. Daddy is making sure of that." I watch the corner of her lips tug upward when she takes a step closer. "No, Tate, I don't regret any of my choices, but I know someone who does."

"Well, considering there's no blood on the walls, I'd say that went better than expected?" Braxton's voice rings out as the door slides closed when he steps out on the balcony.

I'm not sure how long I've been sitting out here, but I know it's been a while because my toes are somewhat numb from the cold. After Farrah left, I needed some air, so I swept the fresh powdery snow off one of the balcony chairs and curled myself into a ball inside my oversized cable-knit sweater.

When I lift my chin from my knees, his sympathetic stare makes my insides coil a little tighter.

"That good, huh?"

"Yeah, *that* good."

"I'm so sorry, Tay." Braxton brushes the snow off the chair next to me before he sits down. I guarantee the remnants of the snow are soaking into his jeans, like they did my leggings earlier. But he doesn't even flinch, unlike me.

"It was bound to happen one day." Still, I had hoped that she'd prove me wrong. Lifting my gaze back toward the sky, I say, "She didn't even try to deny it, and she knew about the gambling and the drugs. She knew everything."

"Did she know about it when she asked you for money?" Braxton asks, and it's silent between us after I nod. The quiet lasts longer than feels normal. The chirp of the birds feels more like a filler than a comforting presence. And slowly, I feel his stare move from the wilderness to me. I should say something else to keep him from digging further, but it's too late. "Did she say anything else?"

I sigh, and my tongue darts out to wet the corners of my lips before I turn to look at him again. "She's getting a payout from her parents after the wedding, and she no longer has to deal with me...So, Farrah is sitting pretty high on the hill, right now."

"That's not what's bothering you, though," he says, and I hate how well he knows me. "What else did she say, Tate?"

I laugh dryly. I know what she said is complete crap, but my mind took it and ran in the one direction I'm sure she intended. Anything to twist the knife a little deeper, to hurt me and cause a little more damage before she walked away for good. Clearing my throat, I ask, "Did you run into each other the morning after you got here?"

"We did."

I bite down on my lip. "She said that when you saw each other, you told her that you missed her and you asked if she ever thought about what life would be like if she had stayed."

His laughter startles me. "I never said that," he says, still chuckling softly. "It was actually Farrah who said it to me."

I roll my eyes. *Of course, she did.*

Braxton reaches over to pull one of my hands into his. "I can honestly say I've never thought about that, and I haven't thought about Farrah Frost in a long time. Once I got over the initial shock…I never thought of her again. There was no reason to. I did my best to move on, to find someone new, but nothing ever worked out."

"Until Micah asked you for money."

Braxton shrugs. "I felt bad for her. If the roles were reversed, I'd want someone to tell me. But I knew it couldn't come from me, because I knew how it would look."

"And that's why you reached out to me," I say, eyes falling to the tops of my knees. If he had been trying to find someone new, that explains why he never reached out to me before. I mean, that's what I had done with Colin. I thought dating him would help me put all of this behind me, to move on from the Farrah and Micah show. But there was always a little piece of me that felt drawn back here—to Snowhaven—and I thought it was because of my family…Now, I think it might have been Braxton this whole time. He was the unwritten part of my story begging to be told. "Did you ever wonder what might happen if we saw each other again?"

"All the time."

There's no hesitation in his eyes or his voice.

"Why didn't you reach out before then?" I ask.

"I didn't think you wanted me to." His thumb grazes over the skin on my wrist, and a shiver runs down my spine—whether from the sensation or the cold, I'm not sure. Even in the sun, the temperature barely reaches above freezing. "Besides, you were still friendly with them, and I wasn't… It didn't seem appropriate. Now c'mon." Standing from his chair, Braxton gently tugs on my hand. "Let's get inside and warm up. You need to finish packing so you can get home in time for Christmas."

"My parents aren't even home," I say, taking a deep breath as I follow his lead. My muscles ache and burn slightly as they work against the stiffness from the cold. "They went on a cruise because I was supposed to be here. Can't say I blame them. A cold one on the beach sounds pretty good right about now."

"Do you want to come with me? I'm sure the family would love to see you."

As much as I'd love to see the Powells, I should go home. Normally, I'd just convince my sister to come over. We could open a bottle of wine and order Chinese takeout, but she went to her boyfriend's this year. "No, I'm going home. I need some time to gather my thoughts before I have to go back to work." I can see the words of resistance sitting on the tip of his tongue. "I'll be okay, Bray. I promise. I just need some space."

"I don't like the idea of leaving you alone on Christmas."

"I'll be fine. And who knows? I might even let you pick me up tomorrow for dinner." For the first time, a real smile slowly creeps across my lips, and he matches it.

"It's a date."

15

"I need more coffee. You want some?" I ask Dad, and he downs what's left in his mug before handing it over. He nods at me briefly before returning to the movie on the television screen. The same one we watch every Christmas, but God save anyone who interrupts his annual viewing.

Mom dries her hands on a kitchen towel as I walk into the kitchen, and meets me at the coffee pot. She crosses her arms, leaning her hip into the counter as she looks up at me with a raised brow. My mother is the shortest person in our family, and my sister isn't too far behind, standing a good eight to nine inches shorter than me. It makes for a sore neck whenever she gives me *that* look she's giving me right now. It's the same one she wore when I first arrived at the house earlier.

My mother greeted me on the front porch this morning with a hot cup of coffee and a knowing smile that quickly morphed into what I like to call the "Mom" look. Macie had spilled the beans about not only my whereabouts, but who I was with. When I walked in, my sister gave me an apologetic smile from the other side of the living room, where she helped her daughter tear the paper concealing her gifts. But no one has said anything yet. We've spent the day watching old Christmas movies while my niece played with her new toys and Mom worked on dinner. And it was everything I wanted out of the holiday, except there was one thing missing...

"So..." Mom draws out the word. My shoulders fall in a heavy sigh. *Here we go.* "I hear you were hanging out with an old friend this week."

"Oh, Ma."

"Don't '*Oh, Ma*' me." She points her finger in my direction. "When were you going to tell me that you and Tate started talking again?"

"There's nothing to tell."

"That's not what I hear," Mom says, a smirk spreading across her lips. I want to lie to her, but I can't. She'd see right through me, just like she always does. Besides, it's not exactly the truth anymore. "When did this start?"

"A few days ago," I admit.

Her brow jumps up, eyes wide. "*Days*?"

"I only reached out to her because Micah is being Micah, doing his normal bullshit. He called me a few weeks ago, asking for money—"

"Braxton." Mom sighs.

"I didn't give him anything. I learned my lesson. And despite what happened between us, I felt like Farrah should know. So, I called Tate to see if she knew anything. We met up for a quick chat, and she left her purse. When I ran up to the hotel to drop it off, one thing led to another, and Farrah invited me to the wedding, thinking that Tate and I were dating."

"Sounds like the makin's of a Hallmark Christmas movie." My mom bites back a grin, and I roll my eyes, earning a slight smack to the arm with the towel. "So, what are you doing here? Shouldn't you be with her at the wedding?"

"We kind of got uninvited."

"We, as in both of you? I thought she and Farrah were best friends."

"Yeah, well, everything between her and Farrah finally came to blows," I say, tracing the rim of my coffee mug.

"Oh, boy." Mom breathes out. "Well, you can imagine my surprise when Macie told me you were up there, not to mention that you were hanging out with Tate. I wish you would've just told me—"

"I'm sorry, Ma. I know I should've called, but things happened so fast. I couldn't tell which way was up." I roll my shoulders and pull the glass pot from the coffee maker, filling both mugs just below the brim. "I didn't plan on getting involved with any of them this weekend, but when I saw her again…everything came back."

"Please tell me that you finally told her all of this."

"We had a few conversations about things."

That's one way to put it.

"And?" Mom plants her hands on her hips. "What did she say?"

"And we're just trying to figure it all out. We haven't put a label on it or anything."

My mother snatches the towel from her shoulder and tosses it on the counter. "Well, seems to me that the universe brought you two back together for a reason. I think you should pack up and head on over to wherever she is tonight. You're not gonna figure anything out sitting right here."

"She asked for some space," I say, leaning back against the edge and tugging on the ends of my hair. "Her parents are out of town, so she has the house to herself and—"

"You mean she's *alone* on Christmas? What is wrong with you, boy?" Mom swats my arm and stops me when I try to argue. "I don't want to hear it. You're going over there this instant. You either take her some food or bring her back, and we'll enjoy a nice family dinner. Together."

Lights hung on the exterior of the house cast a warm, nostalgic glow on the white snow that covers the yard. Smaller trees line the recently shoveled sidewalk, and a larger pine stands at attention to the left on the other end. Giant wreaths with burlap ribbons hang from the sconces on either side of the garage. Two smaller trees that flank the front porch are decorated with dimmed white bulbs, and different sizes of lanterns sit at their bases. Candles with faux flames flicker inside. The curtains of an oversized picture window are pulled, but I know on the other side is a tree covered in rainbow lights, and the room looks like Christmas threw up. Normally, the curtains would be tied back so onlookers could get a taste of the Kerrigan Christmas spirit. I'm shocked she kept them closed.

My feet drag up the sidewalk from the street, each step a little heavier than the last. Even though this is all I could think about since I watched her car drive off this morning, I hate to bother her. She said she needed space, and showing up here unannounced isn't exactly giving her that space.

Walking up the steps, I take a deep breath and knock on the door before I can talk myself out of it. It feels like an eternity before it swings open. Tate is still dressed in the same leggings and oversized sweater from earlier. She has one boot on, and the other in her hand, almost as if I caught her in the middle of putting them on or taking them off.

"Braxton?" she whispers. It's soft and more of a question, like she's trying to decide if I'm really standing here or not. "What are you—"

"I love you." The words roll off my tongue with such ease, it shocks me, and I think her, too. Her brown eyes turn into saucers, and her mouth falls open.

"You lov—"

"I love you, Taylor Kerrigan," I say again, stepping over the threshold. "And I've waited long enough to tell you that." When she doesn't backpedal, I take another step until we're chest to chest. Sweeping her bangs from her face, I cradle her face, her cheeks instantly warming my cold skin. She leans into my touch, eyes closing. "I'm all in, Tay."

Her eyes blink open, and she sighs, trying to take a step back, but I don't let her. "Bray—"

"I know our lives are on completely different paths, but I'm all in. I don't care about any of that. We'll make it work." My thumbs graze over her cheeks, and I smile down at her. "I'm not him, Tate. I want this, I want you, and if you give me the chance, I'll choose you every day for the rest of my life."

Wetness coats her eyes, and the corner of her mouth twitches before she rolls her lips between her teeth. Clearing her throat, she starts to laugh softly. "I love you," she whispers, tearfully, and a weight lifts off my shoulders.

"Say it again," I practically beg, moving in closer to let my lips hover over hers.

Tate chuckles, but does as she's asked. "I love you, Braxton Powell."

"Oh, Pretty Girl, you have no idea how long I've waited to hear that."

EPILOGUE

Tate

SUNDAY, APRIL 25, 2021

TWO YEARS LATER

"Good morning, Mrs. Powell." The words tickle the shell of my ear before his lips press against the side of my face, slowly making their way to find mine in a gentle kiss.

"Good morning, husband," I say with my eyes still closed, and hum in approval when his lips find the sensitive space behind my ear. He smiles before trailing down my jaw and neck. He's woken me up the same way for the past two weeks, since we decided to go to the courthouse and make things official, and I can't get enough. "What time is it?"

"Seven-thirty," he says, and nips at my neck before his tongue soothes the same spot.

"I don't have a lot of time. I have to meet up with Savannah to go over a few things for tonight."

Tonight is Wrestlefest XXXIX in Austin, Texas, and the final chapter in the *Savvy Skye* vs *Kerrigan Tate* story. Over the last two years in the ring, we've gone from friends and tag team partners to EWE Women's Tag Team Champions and ultimately bitter rivals when my character turned on hers at Wreck the Halls last December after we lost the belts. This has been the longest story I've ever been a part of, and now that it's coming to a close, I have to admit I'm a little sad.

"Better tell her you're going to be late."

"Braxton—"

He laughs, and I finally open my eyes to glare up at him. "I'm kidding...kind of."

I shove his shoulder playfully, and he captures my hand in his, bringing it to his lips. It starts with small pecks against each fingertip, then he moves down my wrist and arm, until he pulls my mouth to his.

Braxton wraps his hand gently around my throat, nibbling on my bottom lip, coaxing my mouth open to sweep his tongue over mine. He's taking his time. Time that I don't have, but I find it really hard to care about that when his body covers mine. Savannah will be fine. She'll understand. And if she doesn't...well, that's a problem for future Tate.

A shiver runs down my spine when his fingers release my throat, barely tracing my shape until he reaches my stomach. The skin is exposed by the cropped nightshirt I'd chosen last night. His hand reaches beneath the fabric to knead my breast when his mouth moves again from my lips to my jaw to my ear, pulling the lobe between his teeth.

I moan when he swoops down to take the raised peak he'd just been rolling between his fingers into his mouth through the fabric of my shirt. Fuck, that feels so good. My hand threads through his hair as my back arches off the mattress, my body aching for more. He pushes the shirt up, exposing my bare breasts, and my nipples harden further against the rush of cool air, aching for his touch. Braxton takes the other bud into his mouth this time, sucking and nipping, until I'm a writhing mess beneath him, and he's only just getting started.

"You're a needy thing, aren't you?" Braxton whispers, ghosting his fingers between my legs. A quick pat against my fabric-covered center before he pushes aside my shorts and dips two fingers inside me without warning. He hums in satisfaction, "Fuck, Tay." His fingers scissor inside me before they curl, grazing my most sensitive spot.

"Bray," I whine, moving my hips against his touch.

"Take them off," he demands, and I do as I'm told, watching as he stands to strip off his own sweats. I can't take my eyes off the sharp lines of his torso, the strong muscles that pull taut beneath his bronzed skin. "See something you like?"

I lift my gaze and match the smirk on his lips as he balls up his T-shirt and throws it into the corner.

Braxton climbs onto the bed, pulling my mouth to his before he guides me onto my back. He settles between my legs, grasping his erection to fit the head of his cock to my entrance, and I grasp when he pushes only the tip inside. He rubs up and down my folds, over my clit, and back before finally thrusting all the way in until his hips meet mine, and I gasp.

"I'll never get tired of that," he says.

"What?" It's a bit breathless as he begins to roll his hips.

"The sound you make when I fill you up." Braxton hitches my leg farther up his waist to provide a deeper angle, and I gasp again. "Yes," he moans. "Just like that."

"You're going to make me come if you keep doing that," I say, feeling that tight coil already begin to burn inside my belly.

"Good," is the only thing he says before speeding up his thrusts. With each one, his cock sinks deeper into me, and my nails dig further into the flesh on his shoulders. He stares straight into my eyes, watching me slowly unravel beneath him, until I can't hold on any longer. "Fuck," he hisses when my orgasm peaks, my walls clenching around him. Braxton pulls my mouth to his and continues to thrust hard into me until he's riding the same high.

"She's going to kill me," I murmur when he finally pulls out. His fingers lazily trace a line between the valley of my breasts until they reach the sensitive bud between my legs. I gasp and squirm beneath his touch, trying to get away, but he pulls me back.

"I wasn't done with you yet."

"Bray—"

"You're already going to be late," he says, and rolls my clit between his thumb and forefinger before pushing two fingers inside me. "Five more minutes won't kill her."

Savvy Skye's forearm collides with my chest, and it feels like running straight into a brick wall before I fall back against the canvas. Savannah did that on purpose—a receipt for the unplanned kick to her jaw, not even two minutes ago, that landed probably a little too hard because she wasn't prepared for it when she turned around. She circles the ring, arms spread wide, soaking in the praise from the crowd before reaching down, weaving her fingers into my hair, and forcing me to stand. Without waiting, she tightens her grip, and we run forward into the corner before she slams me face-first into the top turnbuckle.

When I stumble out of the corner, *Savvy* quickly takes hold of my forearm, preparing for an Irish Whip. She attempts to launch me, but I plant my feet, reverse the momentum, and send her flying forward. Her back slams into the corner, and she bounces from the bottom rope to the middle to dropkick me when I run toward her. The momentum sends me stumbling back into the center of the ring. *Savvy* launches herself from the top rope for a crossbody. The impact sends me back down to the mat, but she isn't finished.

She could just pin me, but *Savvy Skye*—the "*Queen of the Ring*"—wants to make an example out of *Kerrigan Tate*. She wants to remind all the women just who they're dealing with.

My opponent climbs back to her feet and forces me from the ground, sweeping her right arm between my legs and lifting me off my feet. She holds me horizontally before dropping down to one knee and slamming my side into it. I cry out against the impact before she tosses me to the mat like a fucking rag doll.

So glad she's not holding back tonight, I think, holding on to my side. Savannah wasn't thrilled that I showed up late this morning, and I can't say I blame her. We only had so much time to walk through the new spots we'd wanted to implement tonight before someone else would need the ring to do the same thing for the match, and I'd wasted at least twenty minutes of our time because I couldn't say no to Braxton.

Back on our feet, *Savvy* pulls my head under her arm, grips the waistband of my shorts, and lifts me over her head onto my back in a suplex. I pop up from the mat, holding my back upon impact, and look up to meet her gaze. Her face is serious, no evidence of the friend I left behind the curtain twenty minutes ago. That's how I should be, too; hell, that's how I normally am, but for some reason, I haven't been able to get out of my head tonight.

Savvy follows me as I roll toward the edge of the ring, grasping onto the bottom rope to try and pull myself up, but she kicks me, knocking me back down. Three more kicks before she uses the ropes as leverage to stand on my throat before the referee yells at her to knock it off. For a moment, she does, backing away with her hands in the air, before doing it again. It only lasts for a brief second before her weight disappears and she rolls out of the ring, dragging me by my hair to the corner.

"*Savvy, what are you doing?*" Jude Paul, the lead commentator, yells from the announcer's table.

Just like we planned, she threads my body under the bottom rope in the corner and takes hold of my leg and neck. When I brought up the idea for this spot, Savannah wasn't sure about it. It was risky. And it could be dangerous if not done properly, but I told her it was fine. Her character is supposed to be on the edge. She is supposed to be toeing the line of good guy and bad guy—a face and a heel—after everything my character *Kerrigan Tate* has put her through, and this would be the perfect way to show it. I trusted her to keep me safe, and I still do as she breathes out and pulls.

I cry out as my back contorts around the steel pole. The angle is awkward and uncomfortable, my body breaking in half as she continues to pull it against the unyielding metal. *Savvy* lifts her foot, leaning into the pole to gain more leverage, and I continue to cry out as my body bends to her will.

"*Knock it off, Skye!*" the referee shouts, and only when he finally begins to count does she let go.

I rub my lower back, applying a small amount of pressure to the sore spot lingering there, before I feel my opponent grab hold of my ankle and drag me into the center of the ring. Contorting my body, I use my free leg to kick her in the abdomen, and she releases her hold. I climb to my feet and barely miss her boot, which flies toward my face. When she turns on her heel, we lock up. I shove her back a step and kick her midsection. *Savvy* doubles over, clutching her abdomen, and I reach for her neck. Snaking my arm around her neck, I twist her body one hundred eighty degrees in a swinging neckbreaker, outstretch my hand for the show of it all, and drop to my seat on the mat.

"*Winter's Kiss!*" I hear Scott Harrington yell out from the commentator's table. *Winter's Kiss* is my most well-known finisher, and most fans expect to see it at least once in any match with the "*Ice Princess.*" I swipe my tongue over my teeth with a smile before blowing a kiss toward the front row.

I shove *Savvy* onto her back and lift her knee, but she kicks out at two. "*C'mon, ref,*" I shout, pushing my hair out of my face. "*That was three!*"

The referee holds up two fingers, and I huff in frustration before pulling my opponent up to her feet.

I whip her into the corner, but she slows her momentum by grabbing the top ropes before she can slam into the turnbuckles chest-first. Planting one foot on the middle rope, she glances over her shoulder briefly as I charge toward her before she climbs. Just before I reach the corner, she launches herself into the air and snakes her arm around my head, pulling me into a DDT position midair. She spins, I'm sure making it look easy and flawless, driving my head into the canvas when we land. The impact stuns me, long enough for her to climb over my body and hook my left leg for the pin. I lift my shoulders and kick out just before the ref slams his hand on the mat for the third time.

Savvy screams out in frustration and takes hold of my head, slamming it into the mat over and over. When she's finally had enough, she falls back onto her heels before slumping into the bottom rope.

It doesn't take long before I feel her fingers secure a tight hold on my hair and force my body up into a bridged position. The soles of my shoes are flat on the canvas, and I cry out when *Savvy* drives her knee into my spine. The crowd counts each one—four in total—before she drops to her knees. Her forearm comes down in a hard strike against my chest— *Heartbreaker*, her signature move. When she's satisfied with the damage done, *Savvy Skye* pushes my shoulders down onto the mat and hooks my leg…

"Now that's what I call a match," Braxton says when I step through the curtain from gorilla. There's a slight twinge in my back from being turned into a human pretzel around a metal pole, and I can't hold back the hiss of pain when my husband squeezes me. "I take it that spot on the pole wasn't as much fun when put into action?"

I glare up at him, hearing the slight smirk in his voice. "I'm fine. Thanks for asking."

"I'm sorry. Let me start over." He clears his throat and gently places his hand on my shoulder. "Are you okay, *Princess*?" Braxton chuckles to himself when I continue to glare up at him, draping his arm over my shoulders to lead me down the hallway. "Sav might have kicked your ass tonight, but you're still a winner in my book. Now let's go get you some ice and ibuprofen."

"How about a massage when we get to the hotel?"

"I think that can be arranged."

Following my loss to *Savvy Skye* tonight, I have to be in Alexandria for *Monday Night Rage* tomorrow before I have the rest of the week off. I'm not scheduled for *Thursday Night Commotion* on Thursday night or the non-televised shows over the weekend, which means after tomorrow night, I'll have six whole days to rest, recover, and annoy my husband. And by rest and recover, I mean head over to Wilder Wrestling Association and work with some of the new wrestlers that Judah recently took in. Guess the old saying is true: You always find your way back home…

Only a few days after everything happened two years ago,

Braxton came home from work and asked if I wanted to join him for dinner with a friend. That friend turned out to be none other than Judah Albright. I found out he had recently taken over WWA from our old boss, Terry, and it just so happened that he needed a new trainer. Without thinking, I accepted. "If you're offering, that is," I said, realizing I had jumped the gun.

"'Course I'm offering. Why else would I bring it up?" Judah rolled his eyes, and a smile tugged on the corners of his mouth. "When can you start?"

And that's how, within the first three months of our relationship, I officially moved back home to Snowhaven Springs, moved in with Braxton, and became one of the trainers at WWA. Not to mention, I was only a few months away from entering into one of the biggest runs of my career at Elite Wrestling Entertainment.

I'm sure you're wondering what happened to our former best friends. Well, I think you'd be happy to know that, according to the *Snowhaven Gazette*, they are thriving in their new marriage and Farrah is pregnant. However, if you were to ask my mom's group of gossips, things aren't as picture-perfect as they seem. Not only did Micah get shipped off to rehab last year—the real deal this time—but he's also been stepping out with Bethany recently. Am I shocked? Not one bit.

"You ready?" my husband asks a little over an hour later when I walk out of the locker room, freshly changed into a pair of sweats and a cropped T-shirt.

Although my match for tonight was finished, I had to stay and watch the main event. *Brooks Taylor* was returning to Wrestlefest main event action for the first time in two years against *Colin Ryker*, and *Wolf Bennett* was set to make a surprise return. His first order of business? Knock *Ryker* on his ass as a thank you for putting him out of commission for six months with an Achilles injury. When he walked through the curtain, *Wolf* looked better than he had in years. I know Brooks was glad to be a part of his best friend's return—Savannah had told me as much—but seeing them work together to dominate their opponent was magical.

Braxton takes the suitcase handle from my hand, sliding his free hand into mine and interlacing our fingers. He gives it a gentle squeeze, guiding me through the maze of hallways to the exit.

I take a deep breath of early spring air when we step out the door, still shielded by the tractor trailers with larger-than-life images of the biggest stars in the company. The one closest to us displays *Rae Rose* and *Wolf Bennett* on one side and *Colin Ryker* and *Cali Kennedy* on the other, the EWE logo in between them.

A roar fills the night air when Braxton pulls me out into the private parking lot reserved for talent cars. Fans line the fence blocking them from gaining access to the lot. I lift my hand in the air and wave at them, but Braxton swats me on the ass. "Go over there. I got the bags."

"Don't you want to leave?"

"We'll leave after you go say hello. Now, go." He kisses my forehead, then gives me a gentle shove.

For the entire ten minutes I spend interacting with almost every person on the other side of the fence, I feel his stare on my back. Before I greet the final two fans, I glance over my shoulder. He leans against the black SUV, legs crossed at his ankles and arms folded. There's an ever-present smile on his face, and it only grows when our eyes meet. With his pointer finger, he makes a small circular motion, telling me to turn around and finish what I'm doing. I roll my eyes, but do as I'm told.

"See, that wasn't so bad," Braxton says when I finally make it back to the car.

Without hesitation, I step into him, wrapping my arms around his neck and pulling his mouth to mine. It shocks him at first, but he chuckles against my lips, returning the embrace.

If you had asked me two years ago if I thought I'd be here right here right now, I would've called you crazy. I guess I have one thing to thank Farrah and Micah for: bringing me and Braxton back together. His love and support are unconditional, and vice versa. Our life together is everything I dreamed of, even during the hard times, but you want to know the best part? It comes with no strings attached.

"I love you, Bray," I say against his lips.

"And I love you, Pretty Girl."

THANK YOU

Did you enjoy *Winter's Kiss*?
Please consider leaving a review on Amazon, Goodreads,
etc!

Interested in more from Jensen Parker?
Scan the code below to sign up for the newsletter

WHAT'S NEXT?

More books in the Elite Wrestling Entertainment series.
Stay tuned for more to come.

You can check out my other books on jensenparker.com!

Acknowledgments

Merry Christmas! I hope you enjoyed this short read, and it helped you get in the mood for the holiday season.

This book was written on a whim. I didn't have any plans to do a holiday book for this year, but after I turned Heartbreaker in to my editor, I sent her a text and asked how much she would hate me if I decided to do a last-minute novella...Her response: "I wouldn't hate you at ALL."

So, here we are.

I couldn't do this without the love and support of the people around me. Thank you for helping me continue to do what I love.

—Jensen ♡

GLOSSARY

Angle A storyline.

Apron A platform area of the ring extends beyond the ropes, covered by a skirt to hide the ring's framework.

Babyface See face.

Body Slam Wrestler lifts opponent and slams them into the mat.

Book To determine and schedule events of a wrestling card.

Botch Something doesn't go as planned. Also, a move that is messed up.

Bump To fall to the mat or the ground.

Call To instruct the other wrestler on what is going to happen in the match. This also refers to the commentators detailing what is happening during a match.

Card The show lineup.

Character See gimmick.

Clothesline A maneuver where a wrestler runs toward their opponent, extending their arm out to the side of their body (parallel to the ground), and striking the opponent in the chest or neck.

Crossbody A maneuver where a wrestler jumps onto their opponent, landing horizontally across their chest or torso, and forcing them down to the mat.

DDT Wrestler places their opponent into a front facelock (aka inverted headlock), and they fall backwards to drive the opponent's head into the mat. This can be done with the opponent's legs hanging from the middle rope.

Drop-kick An offensive maneuver where the wrestler jumps, either off the mat or from an elevated position, and kicks an opponent with both feet.

Face The good guy. (see babyface)

Facebuster
Wrestler forces their opponent down into the mat face-first without a headlock or facelock.

Feud
Staged rivalry between two wrestlers or a group of wrestlers. Feuds may last months or years or be resolved quickly, within the course of a single match, depending on the story.

Finisher
A wrestler's signature move usually leads to pinfall or submission. Sometimes called a "gimmick."

Flying Clothesline
A maneuver where a wrestler runs toward their opponent, leaps into the air, extends their arm out to the side of their body (parallel to the ground), and strikes their opponent in the chest or neck. (see clothesline)

German suplex
Wrestler crouches and wraps arms around their opponent's lower waist (not the chest), then lifts them off the ground until they are overhead. The opponent should continue to fall, landing on the lower part of their neck.

Gimmick
The character portrayed by a wrestler. This involves their in-ring persona, behavior, attire, and distinguishing traits while performing, created to draw fan interest.

Go over
To win a wrestling match.

Gorilla
Headquarters of backstage. The staging area behind the entrance where wrestlers come out to the arena. This is where producers, writers, and other members of the creative process sit during the show.

Heat
Negative reaction from the fans. Also, real-life tension or ill will between two wrestlers.

Heel
The bad guy.

Independent Circuit
A collection of smaller, independently owned wrestling promotions that are not part of major or international organizations.

Independent Promotion
A smaller wrestling company that operates at a local level and usually employs freelance wrestlers. (aka Indie Promotion)

Independent Wrestler
Freelance wrestler, usually not signed to exclusive contracts. (aka Indie Wrestler)

Indies See Independent Circuit.

Irish Whip Not a damaging move, but used to set up for bigger sequences or moves. Wrestler grabs their opponent by the wrist, then pushes them into the ropes or another obstacle. Upon release, the opponent bounces off the ropes or hits the obstacle. Followed up by an attack or counterattack.

Kayfabe The presentation that professional wrestling is entirely legitimate or unscripted. This is not as well-maintained now.

Kick-out To kick or power out of a pin and lift shoulders off the mat.

Legacy Frequently used to describe wrestlers who come from families with deep roots in pro-wrestling.

Mark A wrestling fan who enthusiastically believes professional wrestling is not staged, or loses sight of the staged nature of the business while supporting their favorite wrestler. Often used to refer to people who have little or no knowledge about the business.

Missed Spot A move or series of moves that are mistimed.

Near-Fall When a wrestler's shoulders are pinned to the mat for a two-count, but the wrestler manages to escape before the count of three.

Over When a wrestler achieves the desired crowd reaction, the audience buys into the performer or gimmick.

Pin See pinfall.

Pinfall A wrestler's shoulders are pinned to the mat for a three-count, resulting in a win.

Pop A cheer or positive reaction from the crowd.

Premiere Live Event High-profile wrestling events outside of the normal, weekly programming. These events are often the culmination of long-running storylines and feature highly anticipated matches. (a.k.a. Pay-Per-View [PPV])

Promo An in-character interview or monologue. Typically includes an in-ring or backstage interview or some type of skit by wrestlers to advance a storyline or feud. The act is referred to as "cutting a promo."

Receipt
A term for returning a particularly stiff move in return to a wrestler. This is usually when a wrestler is legitimately hit by their opponent, and they will send a legitimate move/hit back as a wordless reminder not to hit so hard.

Reverse Irish Whip
Not a damaging move, but used to set up for bigger sequences or moves. The wrestler grabs their opponent by the wrist, then attempts to push them into the ropes or another obstacle, but the opponent counters and sends the wrestler into the ropes instead.

Roll-Up
Pinfall maneuver. The wrestler moves behind their opponent, rolling them backwards onto their shoulders for the pin, often grabbing one or both of their opponent's legs.

Running Forearm
A strike where the wrestler runs toward their opponent, leaps into the air, and hits them with their forearm, typically in the upper body.

Running the Ropes
A maneuver where a wrestler rapidly moves across the ring, grabbing the top rope with their hand and leaning into it to gain momentum and spring back into the ring. Often used to set up for a powerful offensive move.

Sell
To react to something in a way that makes it appear believable and legitimate to the audience. Typically refers to the physical action by a wrestler to make their opponent's move look impactful.

Spear
A powerful offensive move where the wrestler charges at their opponent from a distance, then drives their shoulder into the midsection and takes them down to the mat.

Spot
Any planned action or series of actions in a match.

Squared Circle
The wrestling ring.

Standing Dropkick
Wrestler jumps from a standing position and kicks their opponent with both feet.

Stiff
Using excessive force when executing a move, deliberately or accidentally.

Superkick	Wrestler delivers a side kick to their opponent's face or chin, typically with the sole of their foot.
Suplex	Wrestler places their opponent in a front face lock. Wrestler place their opponent's opposite arm over their neck before lifting them off their feet and throwing them backwards, causing them to land on their back.
Takedown	The wrestler brings their opponent from a standing position to the mat.
Turn	A switch in alignment of a wrestler's character. Usually, when a wrestler turns from Face to Heel, or vice versa.
Turnbuckle	A rigging device used to adjust the tension of the ring ropes. There are typically three in each corner, covered in soft pads for the safety of the wrestlers.
Work	(n) Anything planned to happen in a match. (v) To methodically attack a single body part throughout the match. Also, to deceive or manipulate an audience to elicit a desired reaction.

Jensen Parker

Jensen Parker is a wife, mother, and contemporary romance author. She studied English at Loyola University in Chicago and Harvard University in Boston. Coffee, wine, and travel are her love languages (especially when they all coincide!). When she's not working on her next project, she likes spending time with her family, cooking, or planning her next vacation. She currently lives in Indiana.

For sneak peeks, giveaways, and more...Sign up for Jensen's newsletter! https://www.jensenparker.com/subscribe

Follow her on social media!

Instagram : instagram.com/jensenparkerauthor

Facebook : facebook.com/jparkerauthor

Threads : threads.net/@jensenparkerauthor

Twitter : twitter.com/jensenpauthor

Goodreads : goodreads.com/jensenparkerauthor

Amazon : amazon.com/author/jensenparkerauthor

TikTok : tiktok.com/@jensenparkerauthor

"I urge you to live a life worthy of the calling you have received. Be completely humble and gentle; be patient, bearing with one another in love."

- Ephesians 4:1-2

#MadeforMore

www.ingramcontent.com/pod-product-compliance
Lightning Source LLC
Chambersburg PA
CBHW050338110726
47899CB00007B/2551

* 9 7 9 8 9 9 3 1 7 8 1 3 4 *